Praise for Kate Hoffmann's
The Mighty Quinns

"[Kate] Hoffmann always brings a strong story to the table with The Mighty Quinns, and this is one of her best."
—*RT Book Reviews* on *The Mighty Quinns: Eli*

"The [Aileen Quinn storyline] ends as it began: with strong storytelling and compelling, tender characters who make for a deeply satisfying read."
—*RT Book Reviews* on *The Mighty Quinns: Mac*

"[Hoffmann's] characters are well written and real. *The Mighty Quinns: Eli* is a recommended read for lovers of the Quinn family, lovers of the outdoors and lovers of a sensitive man."
—*Harlequin Junkie*

"A winning combination of exciting adventure and romance... This is a sweet and sexy read that kept me entertained from start to finish."
—*Harlequin Junkie* on *The Mighty Quinns: Malcolm*

"This is a fast read that is hard to tear the eyes from. Once I picked it up I couldn't put it down."
—*Fresh Fiction* on *The Mighty Quinns: Dermot*

"As usual, Hoffmann has written a light yet compelling tale with just enough angst and long-term background story to provide momentum for the next member of the Quinn family we are most certainly going to meet."
—*RT Book Reviews* on *The Mighty Quinns: Ryan*

Dear Reader,

When I was a child, my father would regularly spin wonderfully colorful stories for me and my three younger siblings. On Saturday mornings, we'd crawl into bed with my parents and my dad would recollect the time my mother (always the intrepid heroine of these tales) went big-game hunting in Africa or rode an elephant across the Alps.

Is this where I got my storytelling talents? I'm not sure. But I know it's where I got my love for the tradition of a well-told tale. My second novel for Harlequin, published twenty years ago, was a takeoff on the Cinderella fairy tale. And now, eighty-five stories later, I'm about to tell another tale, this one based on *Beauty and the Beast*.

The Quinns are back for another trilogy, featuring "beastly" heros! I hope you'll enjoy!

Happy reading,

Kate Hoffmann

Kate Hoffmann

The Mighty Quinns: Thom

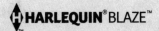

Recycling programs
for this product may
not exist in your area.

ISBN-13: 978-0-373-79905-3

The Mighty Quinns: Thom

Copyright © 2016 by Peggy A. Hoffmann

This edition published by arrangement with Harlequin Books S.A.

For questions and comments about the quality of this book, please contact us at CustomerService@Harlequin.com.

Printed in U.S.A.

www.Harlequin.com

Kate Hoffmann lives in southeastern Wisconsin with her books, her computer and her cats, Princess Winifred and Princess Grace. In her spare time she enjoys sewing, baking, movies, theater and talking on the phone with her sister. She has written nearly ninety books for Harlequin.

Books by Kate Hoffmann

Harlequin Blaze

Seducing the Marine
Compromising Positions

The Mighty Quinns

The Mighty Quinns: Jack
The Mighty Quinns: Rourke
The Mighty Quinns: Dex
The Mighty Quinns: Malcolm
The Mighty Quinns: Rogan
The Mighty Quinns: Ryan
The Mighty Quinns: Eli
The Mighty Quinns: Devin
The Mighty Quinns: Mac

To get the inside scoop on Harlequin Blaze and its talented writers, be sure to check out BlazeAuthors.com.

All backlist available in ebook format.

Visit the Author Profile page at Harlequin.com for more titles.

Prologue

"HE'S GONE! And he's not coming back!"

"Shut up, Thom! Just shut your mouth." His older brother, Tristan, glanced over at the youngest boy in the trio, Jamie. Jamie's eyes swam with tears and Thom cursed himself. The three boys were so close in age that he often forgot that James was still dealing with the fears of a seven-year-old.

Thom reached out and grabbed Jamie's hand, giving it a squeeze. "We'll be all right. We're better off without him. He was just an old drunk who couldn't keep a job."

"Don't say that," Tris warned. "He was our da and we shouldn't talk like that."

Thom wanted to clock his brother. Tristan was almost two years older than Thom, and he understood the reality of their situation. But ulike Thom, Tris was trying to stay positive, hoping that it might keep their mother from losing herself at the bottom of a bottle of vodka.

Life had never been easy for the three Quinn boys,

but Thom knew it was about to get worse. It had begun to unravel three or four years ago, when their da had lost his job. Denny Quinn had started drinking and gambling away the small paycheck their mother brought in. Their parents started fighting more, and a once happy family began to fall apart.

But it hadn't been too terrible until two weeks ago. Until their father had gone out for a pack of cigarettes and hadn't come back. A policeman had come to the door, and Thom had overheard what the man had said to his ma—Denny had been killed during a botched armed robbery, trying to make a getaway after grabbing a wad of cash from an open register.

"At least he won't have to worry about money for food," Thom muttered. Like they did.

"What?" Tris asked.

"Nothing," Thom replied. "It's almost dinnertime. I'm going to go out and get us something for supper."

His gaze met Tristan's and there was a silent agreement between them. Whatever Thom had to do to feed the family was all right. With his mother rarely getting out of bed these last two weeks, it had fallen to him to find food for them. Sometimes he could shoplift enough to feed the four of them. Or he'd find some discarded food in the Dumpster behind a restaurant or grocery store. Occasionally he'd panhandle, but any cash he acquired was saved for other necessities.

"What if Da doesn't come back?" Jamie asked. Thom hadn't been able to bring himself to tell his youngest brother the truth.

Instead, he patted his little brother on the shoulder.

"Don't worry. Me and Tris will always be around. We'll take good care of you and Mum. I promise."

Thom grabbed his jacket and headed to the door of their apartment. The world outside was dangerous, but he'd grown up on the streets. He knew how to get along, how to avoid trouble. And he wasn't afraid to stick up for himself.

He pulled his hood over his head and kept to the shadows, alert for any trouble coming his way. He'd learned the Italian restaurant down the block was a usually a good stop, especially after nine, when the kitchen closed. Leftover pizza, garlic bread, even cold pasta provided a filling meal.

The alley was silent when he arrived. He grabbed an old crate and boosted himself into the Dumpster, searching for a container for his takeout meal. He'd just found a whole pepperoni pizza, only slightly burnt, when the sound of a car engine caught his attention.

He risked a glance out of the bin, then cursed softly. "Cops," he murmured.

A moment later, someone stepped out the back door of the restaurant. "He's in there now," the man shouted.

"Just step back, sir," the officer called as he stepped out of the police car.

Thom tucked the pizza box under his arm and, in one quick move, leaped out of the Dumpster. He hit the ground running. The two men rushed at him, but by the time they crashed into each other, he was half-way down the alley.

He turned to face them, then bent down and grabbed a brick, heaving it at the police car. When it crashed through the rear window, Thom shouted, "Fuck you!" With that, he dashed onto the street, increasing his speed until his lungs burned and he could barely catch his breath.

He could circle back to the grocery store and see if he could snatch a quart of milk or a couple of cans of soda, or he could go home where he'd be safe. Jamie needed the milk, and maybe if his ma had soda, she wouldn't drink the vodka. Thom decided to stash the pizza behind the newspaper box outside a nearby convenience store, then reached for the change in his pocket. It was always best to buy something in the store if he was planning to steal something.

He smiled at the clerk as he walked inside, but the teen barely noticed him, his attention fixed on a small television. Maybe he wouldn't have to buy anything after all. Thom kept his eyes on the other shoppers. He managed to stash the milk, a box of lemonade mix and a block of cheese before he decided to leave.

He walked to the counter and when the clerk turned to him, he smiled again. "My mom wants me to get organic peanut butter. I can't find it."

"We don't have it," the kid said. "Try the grocery store on the next block."

"Thanks," Thom said. He strolled casually to the door, then stepped outside. An instant later, someone grabbed his arm. Thom spun around, throwing his fist out. But he wasn't quick enough. The cop snapped his handcuffs on Thom's wrist.

"Fuck me?" the cop said with a laugh. "Not tonight, buddy. Not tonight."

1

"JUST LET ME do all the talking. If they ask you a direct question, keep your answer short and to the point. Don't try to make excuses. No sarcasm. No attempts at humor. Just be humble and repentant."

Thom Quinn shifted in the front seat of his agent's Porsche, trying to find a comfortable position for his six-foot-three-inch frame. "What do you think they're going to do?"

"Considering your past indiscretions," Jack Warren said, "I think they're going to come down hard. At least a suspension. Maybe a trade."

Thom had played professional hockey for Minneapolis his entire career. A first-round draft pick, he'd spent only one season on their Iowa farm team before being called up late in the year for the playoffs and hadn't looked back. By most standards, he was a star, the kind of player who filled a crucial role in the success of a team. A defensive power who could play both ends of the ice, scoring goals for the Blizzard and blocking shots from the opposing teams.

His on-ice performance had never been in question. He'd exceeded what had been asked of him. But off the ice…he couldn't seem to meet the league standard.

And his latest escapade, three nights before, had been meticulously documented. There were photos of him playing blackjack with two Las Vegas strippers at his side, one of him in a limo with plenty of booze and naked flesh and a cadre of "friends." One of those friends had betrayed him, selling the photos to a tabloid television show. The pictures had then quickly spread throughout the media.

"Can you make this right?" Thom murmured.

"You don't make it easy," Jack said, shaking his head. "You're twenty-seven years old. It's time to grow up, Tommy."

What the hell did that mean? He was on top of his game. He had plenty of cash to spend. Why couldn't he cut loose and enjoy himself now and then? He wasn't breaking any laws. There had been a few scuffles with angry fans and aggressive photographers, a few bitter ex-girlfriends with stories to tell, but he'd always managed to smooth out any problems he'd had with a contrite apology and a generous offer of cash.

Why did he feel the need to push the boundaries of proper behavior? The marketing machine that ran the Minnesota Blizzard had always sold Thom Quinn as a bad boy, a guy who grew up on the streets and came by his tough exterior the hard way. His nickname was "The Beast." They'd created this persona for him, yet they'd never given him a rulebook. How far was too far? Apparently what he'd just done.

But he couldn't leave Minnesota. His family was here and he couldn't abandon them. "I don't want a trade," Thom said. "Promise them whatever they want. I'll take a salary cut. I'll go to rehab. Just make this go away."

"I've heard this all before," Jack said. "Remember last year when you slept with your teammate's ex-girlfriend?"

"They'd broken up," Thom said.

"Alex is your teammate. Did it occur to you what a fight between you might do to the team? Everyone choosing sides? You never think things out, Thom."

"So I'm socially insecure," he replied, an edge of sarcasm in his voice. "I make rash decisions. I constantly try to sabotage myself. I could write a book. I'm sure several of those therapists the team hired have written books about me. I've been told I'm fascinating material."

"Cynicism isn't going to help your case," Jack said.

The car pulled to a stop at a red light, and his agent leaned back into the leather seat. Thom could always count on Jack to be straight with him. And yet Thom had never been able to trust him completely. There were only three people he'd ever trusted in the world— his two brothers and his grandmother. It was a small circle, but it was all Thom had ever needed.

Jack circled the block around the office building that housed Blizzard headquarters, and when he found an empty parking spot, he smoothly pulled the car to a stop. As he switched off the ignition, he turned to

Thom. "Tell me what you want, Tommy. If you want to quit, I'll find a way to make it happen. If you want a trade, we'll get it done. Just tell me what you want."

Thom had been searching for that particular answer since the time he'd walked away from his childhood. Until then, everyone else had made decisions for him. And though he'd fought tooth and nail against any type of authority figure, when his life was finally his own to run, he'd realized he didn't have a plan. His hockey skill was the only thing that kept him from begging for spare change on a street corner. And that wouldn't last forever.

"Maybe you need a fresh start," Jack said. "You could go somewhere and just clear the decks. Start over somewhere else with a new outlook."

"I don't want to leave," Thom murmured.

"You might not have a choice. Of course, we can decide where you might go. Your trade clause gives you final approval. But we'll cross that bridge when we come to it."

As they walked toward team headquarters, Thom drew a deep breath and tried to gather a positive attitude. He'd been through this before—he'd make a stupid mistake, then smooth things over with an earnest apology. His skills on the ice had always balanced the scales. His crimes had been minor, his talent outweighing the consequences.

But he was getting older. He was twenty-seven, and boyish misbehavior wasn't as charming as it used to be. In truth, most of his teammates of the same age were married, some of them with children.

Jack held the front door open for him as he walked into the cool of the air-conditioned offices. Thom straightened his tie, then quickly ran his fingers through his shaggy hair. He'd shaved in an attempt to make himself look a bit more reputable, but he should have taken the time to get a haircut.

When they got to Steve McCrory's office, the receptionist was waiting, a tight smile on her face. She led them both to a nearby conference room. The room was already full, the air thick with tension. Thom cursed softly as he stepped inside. The moment he scanned the occupants, he knew he was in serious trouble.

He'd expected McCrory, the general manager, and Dave Jones, the director of player personnel. But seated at the head of the conference table was Davis Pedersen, the team owner, a formidable figure at the best of times, but now he wore a stony expression on his face.

Thom heard a soft sigh slip from Jack's mouth. This was much more serious than he'd anticipated. Pedersen stood as they entered and pointed to a pair of chairs. "Take a seat, gentlemen."

A ringing in Thom's ears muffled the sounds of the voices around him. Other people arrived and sat down at the table, some faces familiar, some not. Thom's gaze settled on a slender blonde who sat on the opposite end of the table. She was the only woman in the room, so it was hard not to notice her.

Her gaze met his, her pale blue eyes lingering for a moment. Thom sent her a halfhearted smile and she returned the favor. She seemed the only one in the room, besides his agent, willing to look him directly in the eye. Another bad sign.

The conversation began and Thom listened silently as all of his faults were recounted, one by one, each followed by a short dissertation on how his actions had negatively affected the image of both the league and the team.

He didn't attempt to defend himself, or explain. Instead he waited for his turn to speak, knowing they'd expect some type of apology before they moved on to the punishment.

Finally Thom opened his mouth, ready to be humble. But Davis Pedersen held up his hand. "I don't want to hear your excuses or your apologies. Hell, I don't even want a promise that you'll start to behave in a manner befitting the position you hold. As far as I'm concerned, those would all be empty words. You've made promises in the past, and you've broken them all. So, Mr. Quinn, here's how this is going to play out. I plan to trade your ass to the first team that pays me a decent price. Until then, I expect you to behave like a choirboy, and I will do whatever it takes to make sure that happens. If you fight me on this, I'll send you to the worst damn team in the league."

Jack cleared his throat. "We have a trade approval clause, so you'd have to—"

"I don't have to do anything," Pedersen snapped. "Your boy has broken his morals clause more times than I can count." He tossed a file folder across the table at Jack and the agent pulled a photo from it.

"The girl sitting beside you in this photo is a teenage hooker," Pedersen said. "This is going to be posted on—on—what the hell is it called?"

The blonde cleared her throat. "Instagram."

"Right. We were contacted by a bartender at your hotel in Vegas. He informed us that this…girl has been kicked out of the place repeatedly for soliciting. And she's underage. He wanted five thousand or he's going to post the photo on the internet."

"I can explain that photo," Thom said.

Davis slammed his palms down on the table, his expression fierce. "I don't want a damn explanation. I want you to exercise some self-control!" Pedersen stood. "We're done here. If you'll excuse us, we have some plans to discuss."

Pedersen led the other men in suits out of the room, but the blonde hung back. "Can I get you something to drink?" she asked Thom. "Coffee. A soda, maybe?"

"Do you have any arsenic?" Thom asked.

She laughed softly. "No. I'm afraid not. Even if we did, I'm sure I wouldn't be authorized to give it to you."

"I'm all right," he said.

"I hope so," she replied. "Good luck. I hope it works out for you."

"Thanks," Thom said, taking a long look at her. Who was she? She must work for the team. But doing what? He hadn't seen her at the rink; he would have remembered someone so beautiful. Hell, if he had met her, he would have found some way to seduce her. He usually didn't let an attractive woman get past him.

"Don't even think about it," Jack muttered as the woman left the room.

"What? I'm not thinking about anything," Thom lied. "She's pretty. Who the hell is she?"

"You don't know?" Jack asked. He shook his head and chuckled. "Probably for the best."

"No, really. Who is she?"

"She's Malin Pedersen. Davis Pedersen's only daughter."

"I thought his daughter was still in high school."

"She was. When you were drafted. She's grown up."

"She's pretty," Thom said. "What did you say her name was?"

"Malin."

"Kind of a weird name," he murmured.

"I believe it's Swedish," Jack replied.

"Malin," Thom whispered to himself.

A beautiful name for a beautiful woman. He drew a deep breath and scolded himself inwardly.

"Exercise some self-control!"

His boss's command echoed in his head. Yes, it was definitely a bad idea to imagine the boss's daughter naked and lying in his bed...

"THIS IS YOUR FAULT," Davis Pedersen said, scowling at his daughter from across his desk as she and Steve McCrory followed him into his office.

"How is this my fault?" Malin asked.

"I hired you to contain all this Flitter business. We never had these kinds of problems in the past. Now the moment one of our players steps out of line, there's someone there to take a photo and blast it all over the internet."

"It's Twitter," Malin said. "And I can only control our players and what they post. I can't control the whole world."

"Then what good are you? I don't understand how something as ridiculous as that damn Flitter—"

"Twitter," Malin corrected him again.

"What?"

"It's called Twitter. Instagram. Snapchat. Skype. Tinder. Didn't you read the handbook I wrote for the players?"

"I don't need a damn handbook to tell me what's happening to the reputation of my team, and this man is dragging it into the gutter with him. I want him watched 24/7. Until we work out a trade, I want Thom Quinn on complete lockdown, and I'm putting you in charge of that. If there is even a hint of trouble—if a single photo of him is put on *Twitter*—this job you created for yourself is done and you can head back to your fashion designer friends in New York."

Malin gasped. "You're the one who begged me to come home and handle this problem for you. You said if I wanted a role in the organization, I'd have to prove myself."

"And so you will," her father said. "Protect my investment."

Malin turned to Steve McCrory. "Are you really planning to trade him? He's one of our best players. And the fans love him. I'm sure I can smooth this over. Just give me a little time."

"We can't continue to let his off-ice behavior bring negative publicity to the club," McCrory said. "He's gone from drunken brawls to teenage hookers. What's next? I don't want to wait to find out. It was my decision to trade him, and your father backs me on that."

"I don't agree," she said. "If you want to see a social media firestorm, wait until you announce this trade."

"Once we trade him, he'll be someone else's problem. Until then, he needs a watcher."

It was useless to argue. When it came to decisions about the team, McCrory was an immovable force. He was backed by her father, and there was no hope of changing his mind.

She couldn't blame her father. When he bought the franchise seventeen years before, it was a failing enterprise with the lowest attendance figures in the league. Now the club led the league in season ticket sales, merchandising and number of playoff appearances. Though they'd fallen short in the championship series last month, they were poised to make another run next year.

"I can turn him around," Malin said. "I've got two months before training camp starts. Give me a chance. Maybe I can find a way to redeem him."

"My mind is made up," McCrory said.

"Mine, too," her father added. "Why don't you go explain what we expect of him these next few weeks?"

"Me?"

"I said he needs a watcher. That's you. Or are you not up for the challenge?"

"Of course. You won't regret putting this faith in me."

Malin walked out of her father's office, her spirits deflated. She'd never really believed that her father wanted her to work for the team. It had always been an old boys' club, not an atmosphere welcoming to women. But women made up 45 percent of their audience, a figure that was growing with every year that passed. Sooner or later, the old guys would need to admit that they needed a woman in the executive offices. And she was determined that woman would be her.

She found Thom Quinn where she'd left him in the conference room. She glanced over her shoulder as she entered. "Did your agent leave?"

Quinn shook his head. "No. He had to take a call."

Malin pulled out a chair at the end of the table and grabbed a phone, punching in the number of her assistant. "Leah, I'm in the conference room. Can you find Jason and have him come in here? He's probably in the mail room, working on the convention mailing."

She hung up the phone and met Thom Quinn's gaze, holding it for a moment longer than seemed proper under the circumstances. Malin swallowed hard. What were the circumstances? She wasn't his boss. She didn't have any power over him, at least none that didn't come directly from her father. What if he refused to do as she said? In one quick stroke, she'd lose the last of her credibility with her father and any shot at a management job with the team.

"So, they sent you to give me more bad news?"

"Bad news?"

"Yeah, that they've decided to trade me to the worst team in the league?"

"Yes," she murmured, her gaze still locked on his. "I—I mean, no."

He was an incredibly handsome man. That had always been part of his appeal to the female fans. The shaggy dark hair. The scruffy beard. The impossibly blue eyes. Added to that was a collection of imperfections that made him irresistible—the scar on his lip, the slightly crooked nose.

Dragging her eyes from his face, she reached out and straightened her pen sitting beside her notepad.

"Which is it?" he asked. "Trade or no?"

Malin drew a deep breath. "No," she lied. She was still determined to save him. He'd be much more amenable to her plan if he thought he had a chance to stay. "They're going to give you another chance."

He frowned. "Really?"

Malin nodded. "Under some conditions," she said.

"What would those be?"

"Maybe we ought to wait for your agent."

"No, please. Give me my punishment. I'm willing to do what I have to do to stay with the team."

"All right," Malin said. "There'll be no more drinking in public. And I'd advise no more drinking at all. You make stupid decisions when you drink."

He stared at her silently and she paused for a moment, waiting for a comment or a refusal. But when he said nothing, Malin forged on.

"You should also probably take a break from the women, too. I don't mean to say you can't date, but consider keeping your private life more...private." She cleared her throat. "And finally, we're going to assign you a—a personal assistant." It sounded so much better than a watcher, she thought to herself. "This person will live with you and help you make the proper choices and—"

"You're assigning me a babysitter?" he asked.

"Of course not. You're not a baby. You're a full-grown man with a lot of decisions to make. Which is why you need a personal assistant."

He chuckled softly, shaking her head. "All of this because of one photo?"

"If we hadn't killed that photo, you could have ended up in jail."

"I knew she was a hooker," he said. "And that she was underage."

"What?" Malin asked.

He nodded. "She approached me in the bar. She looked hungry and scared. She had a black eye and a swollen lip. We started to talk and it was obvious she could do with a meal and a decent night's sleep. So I bought her dinner and rented her a room. The next morning, I stopped by her room and gave her money to go home. She took it, and as far as I know, she's back in Kansas or Nebraska or wherever she came from. I guess the guy must have snapped a picture when we were in the bar."

"You didn't..."

"I do have some limits when it comes to my behavior."

"Why didn't you say anything?"

He grinned and shrugged. "I tried, but they wouldn't

listen. Besides, it wouldn't have mattered. They see me the way they want to see me."

She studied him silently. Malin had read his bio, the rags-to-riches story—he'd been a juvenile delinquent, virtually orphaned and living on the streets before stumbling into an after-school hockey program.

He'd never had a steady male influence in his life. Instead, he'd been forced to cobble together the rules and expectations of adulthood. Add to that the quick acquisition of wealth and fame and it would mess anyone up. But was she really prepared to untangle that mess? If it meant gaining a whole lot of respect, damn right she was.

"Miss Pedersen?" said a voice from behind her.

Malin turned to see her second cousin, Jason, waiting nervously at the door. His mother had sent him to the Twin Cities when he'd failed to find a job after five years in college. He hadn't impressed her beyond his ability to overthink nearly every project he'd been given. But Malin needed someone who'd take the job seriously, someone who'd stick to Thom Quinn like glue.

"Jason Pedersen, this is Thom Quinn," Malin said.

"I—I know who you are," Jason said. "I met you last spring at the fan convention. You signed my helmet."

"Mr. Quinn, I'm going to suggest you hire a personal assistant. One who'll live with you 24/7. I trust you can make a place for him at your home. Of course, the team will provide a stipend for his rent."

"You want me to live with someone?" Thom asked.

"This is nonnegotiable," Malin said. "Perhaps we should discuss this with your agent?"

"No," he said. "It's fine with me."

"You'll also pay his salary," Malin added.

"I will?"

"Yes. Due to contract restrictions, we can't force you to hire an assistant. We can encourage you to do it on your own, though. Which I'm now strongly suggesting." She leaned forward, her hands splayed across the conference table. "Please do it, Mr. Quinn. Trust me, if you want to keep your job, you need to do this."

Malin waited, knowing that her ability to sway his behavior was key to her plan working. If he fought her, then it was going to be a very difficult summer for them both.

"All right," he finally said. "I can make room for Jason."

Jason gasped. "What? Me?"

"You're going to be Thom Quinn's new personal assistant," Malin said.

Jason's eyes went wide. "I'm moving in with Tommy Quinn? I'm moving in with The Beast?"

"We're not going to be using that nickname anymore," Malin said. "Call him Mr. Quinn for now."

"You can call me Thom," he said, nodding at Jason.

At that moment, Thom's agent returned to the room, his phone still held up to his ear. "What's happening?"

"I've just hired a personal assistant," Thom said in a bright tone. "This is Jason. He's going to help me get my shit together."

Jack glanced back and forth between his client and Jason. "That's it?"

"Yeah," Thom said. "He's going to be living with me. I think it will work out just fine. Jeff and Jake both have assistants, and they say it's great. Maybe he can also do my laundry? And clean the fridge? It will be nice to have a workout partner." He stood, then held out his hand to Malin. "If we're finished here, I'll meet Jason at my place. You can give him the address and send him over with his stuff."

The moment their hands touched, Malin felt a current race through her body. Thom's hands were strong, his fingers long and slender. He was known for his great hands, but she'd assumed that referred to his stick handling abilities. She stared down, her mind suddenly occupied with thoughts of what his hands might do to her body. Great hands indeed. A shiver raced through her.

"What about you?" he murmured. "How will you know that I'm complying with your wishes?"

"I'll be in daily contact with Jason, and he'll keep me up to date on how you're doing. You'll be expected to work out with a team trainer and skate every day. We'll put together a schedule."

"All right, then," Thom said. He suddenly let go of her hand, and Malin wondered if she'd ever have the chance to touch him again.

She watched him follow his agent out of the conference room, then flopped down into one of the leather chairs.

She was acting like a puck bunny, getting all flushed

and breathless the moment she set eyes on a handsome hockey player. This had never happened to her before. Why was it happening now?

"He is so cool," Jason said. "The Beast! How can you not like that guy?"

Malin was wondering the exact opposite—how could she *stop* liking him?

Thom stood in front of the open refrigerator door and examined the contents. Old takeout containers, a few packages of hot dogs, juice, vitamin water and beer. Though he worked hard to maintain a decent diet, it was much easier during the season when meals were provided by the club's caterer.

"Can you cook?" he called.

"Cook?" Jason wandered into the kitchen area. "Sure. Pizza. Mac and cheese. Man, your place is so cool. What guy wouldn't love living in an old firehouse? Was it like this when you moved in?"

"No, I renovated it myself." Thom grabbed a couple of beers, starting to make a grocery list in his head. McCrory and Pedersen had made it clear they wanted him to lay low for the next couple of months, so he wouldn't be dining at his favorite restaurants. He followed the sound of Jason's voice to the family room at the rear of the house.

Jason had already found the remote for the television and was flipping through the channels. "You are old enough to drink, aren't you?" Thom asked before handing the other man the beer.

"I'm twenty-two. But I probably shouldn't drink since I'm on duty."

Thom grabbed the remote and switched to the local sports report. "We need groceries. You might as well hit the store. While you're gone, I'm going to take a run."

Jason shook his head. "I'm not supposed to leave you alone. If you need me to shop, then you have to come with me. If you're going for a run, I go with you. That's what Malin told me and I'm not going to screw it up. I'm supposed to stick to you like glue on rice." He cleared his throat. "Or maybe it was white on rice. Yeah, yeah, that's it. White on rice. Flies on flypaper."

"All right. We can send out for a pizza," Thom muttered, stretching his legs out in front of him. "Why don't you go grab a bedroom and unpack your stuff?"

"I can do that later. I—I'm just gonna sit here and watch the sports report."

"I'm not going to sneak out while you're upstairs."

"No, no," Jason said. "I trust you. Completely. Why don't I call for the pizza? Malin—I mean, Miss Pedersen—gave me some cash. My treat."

"Malin," Thom repeated. "You call her Malin?"

"Not around the office. But she's my cousin, so it would be weird to call her Miss Pedersen any other time."

"What else did she tell you?"

Jason shrugged. "Just…stuff."

"Like what?"

"She said I shouldn't let you drink. That I should keep you away from sleazy women. I'm supposed to work out with you every day, and if I can get you to read an actual book, she'll give me a bonus."

"She expects you to do all that? She must be tough to work for."

"Nah, she's really nice. I've screwed up a few times—more than a few times—and she always gives me another chance."

"What else do you know about her? Does she have a boyfriend?" He handed Jason the beer and this time the other man took a sip, his earlier reluctance forgotten.

"I think she used to. Someone said he used to come to the games, but he lived in New York. That's where she used to live before she came back to Minneapolis." He shrugged. "I've never seen her with a guy. I'm pretty sure she likes men. I've just never…"

"What's her job?"

"Social media. She runs the team website and all the social media accounts. She filters the team's Twitter posts and Instagram photos. So if you post something that would reflect badly on the team, she catches it before it goes out."

"I don't do social media," Thom said.

"Yeah, I know. You make up for it with all the other stuff that gets posted about you. God, I wish I had your social life. All those beautiful women. Maybe you can give me some advice?"

"Where does she live?"

"Malin? She's got a place in Merriam Park. I've only been there a few times. Just to check on the place while she was out of town. It's nothing like this place. Just an ordinary house."

Thom let those few nuggets of information roll around in his mind for a bit, curious about the woman who suddenly held so much power over him. He wanted to dig deeper, to find out every little detail about her. What did she eat for breakfast? Did she sleep in pajamas or the nude? Did she—

Thom stopped himself. This was exactly the kind of thought pattern that had gotten him into trouble in the past. Once he'd decided he wanted a woman, there was nothing that stood in his way. It didn't matter how long it took or what he had to do to get her into bed. In the end, he always made it happen.

A voice from the TV caught his attention. "A late-breaking report regarding your Minneapolis Blizzard."

Both Jason and Thom turned to look at the television.

"Trade rumors are swirling, and at the center of the storm is Blizzard defenseman Tommy 'The Beast' Quinn. Sources say his off-ice shenanigans haven't been sitting well with team's owner, Davis Pedersen. Is Quinn on his way out? Fans are not going to be happy. We'll have an exclusive on our late report."

Thom stared at the television for a long moment. With a soft curse, he shut the television off and tossed the remote on the coffee table. "She told me I wasn't going to be traded," he muttered. Launching to his feet, he turned to Jason, looming over him in his most threatening manner. "What do you know about this?"

"I—I— Nothing. They don't tell me anything. I swear."

"Come on. I want you to show me where she lives.

Miss Pedersen and I have some things to discuss."
Thom shoved his hand in his pocket and pulled out
the keys for his truck. When Jason didn't move, he
said, "Don't you have to go with me?"

"She's probably still at the office," Jason said.

"I'm not going to talk to her there."

"You can call her," Jason suggested. He held out
his cell phone.

Thom shook his head. "No, this has to be done in
person. Why would she lie to me? I mean, I went in
there fully expecting to be traded. And then she decides to put me through this crap. Locked up like a
prisoner with you reporting my every move. What's
that all about?"

"I don't know," Jason said. "But I do know that if
I show you where she lives and you go there, she's
going to fire me. Can you just sit down and we'll order
a pizza?"

"No," Thom snapped. "I want this settled now."

He walked to the front door, not bothering to wait
for Jason. When he reached his truck, parked on the
street, he got inside. As he slipped the key into the ignition, Thom heard a rapping on the window. Jason stood
at the passenger door, a stricken expression on his face.

Thom unlocked the door and the kid hopped inside.
"I can show you where she parks. We could wait for her
there. She always leaves the office at five. If she has to
work late, she comes back after dinner."

"Five," Thom said. They had fifteen minutes to
make a ten-minute drive. At least it would give him a
bit of time to figure out exactly what he wanted to say.

Hell, he should have known not to trust her. She wasn't on his side. She was the daughter of the damn owner. Of course she'd side with her father. Well, he was going to fight this trade. Why lie down and let the team walk all over him? If he wanted to, he could make things very difficult for them.

He knew there was a morals clause in his contract, a section that directly addressed bad behavior. Beyond his youthful criminal record, Thom's "rap sheet" was long and colorful. The brawls—with fellow players, with fans, with bartenders and limo drivers and bouncers and parking attendants—were probably the most egregious.

The women followed a close second. Though they didn't cause as much legal trouble as the brawls, they were a distraction, especially when one decided to spill her secrets to a gossip website.

Until recently, Thom had been able to keep the drinking pretty much under control. But now, there seemed to be more reasons to drink than reasons not to. It wasn't just something he did to relax anymore. Getting drunk was the only way he could shut off the constant hum in his head, turn off all the questions rattling round in his mind.

Life used to be pretty simple for him. He played hockey and he did it better than almost everyone in the league. It provided for him and his family. But now, it seemed that with every year that passed, his life grew more complicated. What would he do when he couldn't play hockey anymore?

Thom had vowed that he'd get out of the game

gracefully. He never wanted to be one of those guys who hung around trying to recapture lost glory. He wanted to go out on top. But how could he be sure the time was right? And what would he do once hockey was over for him?

"It's right here," Jason said, pointing to the parking ramp.

Thom turned into the entrance and grabbed a ticket, then steered the truck up the levels. "What kind of car are we looking for?"

"She has a dark green Audi. It's usually on the fourth level."

Thom found the car and pulled into a spot across the aisle from it. He shut off the truck, then nervously tapped the steering wheel with his fingertips. "What time is it?"

"A few minutes before five. She should be coming along any minute." Jason slouched down in the seat. "What are you going to say to her?"

"I don't know," Thom said. The drive over had been too short to untangle the knot of emotions in his gut.

"Don't you think you'd better figure it— Wait. Someone's coming."

"Is it her?"

"Yeah, it is."

They each watched in their side view mirrors as Malin strolled past. Thom reached for the door and then, at the last minute, decided to wait. "She's gorgeous," he murmured.

"You think so?" Jason asked.

"Don't you?"

"Well, she's my cousin, so I really don't look at her that way. And I'm really more attracted to brunettes than blondes."

Malin got into her car and slipped behind the wheel. Thom held his breath, waiting for just the right moment. When she began to back out of the parking spot, he knew the moment was at hand, and yet he couldn't bring himself to get out of the truck.

He didn't want their next encounter to be an argument. And he certainly didn't want it to happen in a parking lot with Jason looking on.

"She's driving away," Jason said.

"Yeah."

"I don't get it. Everybody says you're legendary with women," Jason murmured.

"Most of that is just talk," Thom said. "Most of the time I have no idea what the hell they're thinking. Or what I'm doing." He reached for the ignition. "You know what? I could use a drink. Let's go to a bar."

"I'm not supposed to—"

"Jason, if we're going to get along, you're going to need to learn that the rules just don't apply to us. Got it?"

2

SLEEP DIDN'T COME easily that night for Malin. Her head was filled with memories of the day's events, which led to her mind weaving tantalizing little fantasies about Thom Quinn.

She'd never been attracted to one of the hockey players before, and she couldn't explain this sudden attraction to Quinn. By all accounts, the guy was a mess. Yet it was hard to ignore his physical perfection, the handsome features, the unruly hair, the body that had been carved out of solid muscle.

After their meeting, she'd shut herself in her office and searched the internet for any information about him that wasn't included in his personnel file. She came across plenty of shirtless photos, both professional and candid, along with a fair number of pictures of Quinn and his women. There were even a few of him when he was younger, hockey photos that showed a sweet-looking boy with a chipped front tooth and a ragged haircut.

She knew that unlike most of the league's star players, Thom Quinn hadn't laced on his first pair of skates until he was twelve. He'd struggled at first but quickly learned the game. It provided a lucky alternative to the street life that he'd been drawn to.

On the ice, Quinn was confident and strong, in command of all his talents and skills. But once he stepped off, he seemed to have nothing to hide behind, and his life fractured at the slightest stress. She realized he was still that screwed-up kid from the streets. Why was she the only one who recognized that fact?

She groaned softly and pulled the pillow over her head. This was crazy. The guy would probably be on a plane out of town by next week and she was quickly turning him into her imaginary boyfriend.

The sound of her cell phone ringing was muffled by the pillow. She threw it off the bed, then sat up and grabbed her phone. Jason's number came up on the screen, and Malin fumbled to answer.

"Hi, Jason. What's—"

"He's gone," Jason said, his voice wavering slightly. "We were just hanging out, watching a Cubs game, and I—well, I kinda—lost track of him. Just for a few minutes."

"How long?"

"Since about nine. I thought he'd be back after the bar closed, but that was an hour ago."

"You were in a bar?"

"We just stopped for a drink after we— Never mind. I tried to talk him out of it, but then we started playing dice and drinking shots and I got totally wasted."

"Where are you now?"

"At his place. I'm so sorry. I tried to say no, but he's very persuasive."

"All right, just stay where you are. I'll be there in a few minutes. Have you tried calling his cell phone?"

"He doesn't answer. Do you think he might have been in an accident?"

"No, no! I'll be there in a few minutes." She turned off her phone and tossed back the bedcovers. It shouldn't have been any surprise that it had taken Thom Quinn less than a day to break the rules.

She crawled out of bed. When she reached the bathroom, Malin ran a comb through her tangled hair and took a few extra seconds with her makeup, then pulled on a pair of yoga pants and a loose shirt.

Five minutes later she was on the road, and ten minutes later she pulled up in front of Thom Quinn's place. At first she had to recheck the address. She was parked in front of an old firehouse. But when Jason appeared on the sidewalk, she knew she'd found the right place.

"I can't do this job, Malin," he said, pacing the sidewalk. "How am I supposed to sleep? And if he decides to go somewhere without me, how can I force him? He could just punch me and knock me out or—"

"Get you drunk?"

"Exactly! I think you picked the wrong person for this job. I'm just not ready."

"Maybe we could put a bell around his neck," she muttered as she stepped inside the front door. She dropped her bag on a nearby table, then slowly began to explore the house. "Wow," she said with a gasp. "This place is—"

"I know," Jason said. "He did all this himself. He's my hero. If I could do something like this, my father would think I was amazing. He'd probably talk to me again."

"Jason, why don't you take off. I can handle this on my own. It would probably be better if you weren't here when Thom got back."

"Am I fired?" Jason asked.

"No. Just reassigned. This one was always going to be tricky. It just turned out to be more difficult than I thought."

"Tommy's angry because he saw on the news that they're going to trade him. He said you lied to him. Is he going to be traded?"

She shrugged. "Probably. But I'm going to make the case for him to stay if he'll cooperate and if I can get a few more people to back me. It could be our little project."

"Why are you doing this?"

"Because if I were the general manager of this club, I'd find a way to turn him into a hero off the ice as well as on it. He can be fixed, and I'm the one to do it. And when it's time for me to run this club, people will remember how I saved Tommy 'The Beast' Quinn."

Jason laughed. "You want to be general manager? That's pretty funny."

She gave him a withering glare, shaking her head. "Would you like to rethink that statement?"

"Sorry," Jason said. "I'll just be going."

"Can you drive?"

He nodded. "I really am sorry. And I promise, I'll make it up to you."

Malin walked Jason to the front door, then locked it behind him. Leaning back against the wood, she closed her eyes and drew a deep breath. With Jason acting as a buffer, it would have been easier for her to keep a professional distance. But less than twenty-four hours after reaching an agreement with Thom, he'd broken it—and she was forced to step in. It was clear he needed a firmer hand, a more determined personality.

Malin wasn't about to let one little bump in the road deter her. She wouldn't stop until she'd achieved her goal. She'd tame The Beast or die trying.

Proving her worth to her father had been a lifetime challenge. Her older brothers had it easy. Hockey was a natural fit for them, and they'd played from the time they could balance on skates until they'd been brave enough to quit. The eldest, Daniel, was now a resident in cardiac surgery, and her other brother, Kristian, worked as an attorney for the US Justice Department. They had no interest in running the team. But the moment her father had called, she'd left a prestigious job in New York to take her chances with the team.

She walked back to the kitchen, taking in the details of Thom Quinn's home. It certainly wasn't what she'd expected. Most of the single guys on the team lived in one of the city's luxury high-rise condos. But Thom's home showed his artistic side. He was obviously good with his hands. Malin groaned. His hands again. She couldn't seem to stop thinking about his hands.

She tried to refocus on his home. The place had

never been profiled in any of the city's glossy magazines, even though it deserved to be. With her media contacts, she could get an article placed in the next few months.

She wandered through the old fire station, taking in all the details, trying to imagine how a photographer might shoot it.

The cream-colored brick walls were exposed throughout the entire building, and massive wood beams supported each wall. At one time the lower level must have housed horses, because Thom had left the old sliding doors in place.

She paused just inside his bedroom door, wondering if her tour ought to stop there. She was interested in the decor, but there were too many other things that came to mind when she glanced inside his bedroom.

The room was huge, spacious and airy, with a huge bed against one wall. She took a few steps further so she could see inside his bathroom—floor-to-ceiling dark gray marble with a steam shower and a whirlpool tub. Her curiosity got the better of her, and she crossed to the line of bottles on a glass shelf beside the sink.

The cologne held a hint of citrus with a tantalizing cover of musk. She smiled as she set the bottle back in place.

"You're the last person I expected to see here."

Malin jumped at the sound of Thom's voice, the bottle clattering against the glass shelf. She spun around to find him watching her from the doorway of the bathroom. He leaned casually against the doorjamb, his arms crossed over his chest.

Malin held her breath as he slowly crossed the room to stand beside her. He stared at her in the mirror. "Jason called you?"

She nodded. "You got him drunk?"

"He did that all on his own." Thom paused. "Besides, he wasn't cut out for the job. He's too young, too impressionable."

"You got him drunk to prove a point?"

"I just couldn't live with the guy," Thom admitted. "He's like a big drooling puppy. I need someone a little more interesting. More mature. With less drool."

"All right. We'll find someone else. I can contact an agency and they'll send over some candidates."

"I can think of an excellent candidate," he said. "Perfectly qualified. Interesting to talk to. Stubbornly disciplined. Beautiful to look at."

"You want a woman?"

He gave her a boyish grin. "I want you." He leaned closer and grabbed her hand. "The question is, do you want me?"

She drew in a sharp breath and tried to control the pounding of her heart. This was crazy. But it could be a great opportunity. If she was with him full-time, she might have a chance at succeeding in taming The Beast.

But was he making the offer because he truly wanted her help? Or was he interested in something else? Something that had nothing to do with business or professionalism or…

Still, she had to take that chance.

"If I agree to do this, you have to do exactly what I tell you. You have to trust me completely."

"Why should I trust you if you don't give me the truth?" he asked.

"I told you, the team—"

"Not about that. You didn't answer my question." He leaned closer and she held her breath. "Do you want me?"

"The truth and you'll trust me?"

"Exactly."

His lips were just inches from hers, and Malin fought the impulse to close that distance and kiss him. "Yes," she breathed.

His kiss was tentative at first, his lips just barely brushing hers. But then he slipped his hands around her waist and pulled her closer, and she felt the warmth of his tongue.

Malin had been kissed by a variety of men in her past, but she'd never experienced a kiss that was so perfect. Just the right mix of overwhelming passion and unspoken desire.

When he finally drew back, she couldn't help but sigh, wishing that it might have gone on for a bit longer.

"Well?"

She opened her eyes to find him staring down at her, his expression cool, his lovely mouth set in a hard line. Malin cleared her throat. "It was…nice." She swallowed hard. "Quite pleasant. But if I'm going to take the job, we can never do that again." She snatched her hand away and rubbed her palm against her hip. "You have to promise."

"I've never been very good with promises," he said, his voice low and rough. Thom reached out and smoothed his fingertips across her cheek. "I'm tired. I need some sleep. We'll talk more in the morning."

As he walked away, he pulled his shirt over his head and tossed it aside. Malin hurried after him into the bedroom. She stopped short as she watched him skim his jeans down over his hips and kick off his trainers. When he reached for the waistband of his boxer briefs, she quickly turned her back.

"If we're going to be living together, you should probably get used to this."

Get used to what, exactly? Malin wondered. Get used to seeing him half-naked? Get used to hanging out in his bedroom at night? Get used to wondering what it would be like if she allowed him to kiss her again? There were so many things racing through her mind, she couldn't imagine what he meant.

"I'll just say good night," she murmured. "And see you in the morning." She risked one last glance at him as she hurried out of the room. It was enough to glimpse him in all his naked glory, with broad shoulders, a narrow waist and muscular backside, before he slipped beneath the covers.

She pulled the bedroom door shut behind her, then hurried back to the living room. She stood in the center of the dimly lit room, waiting for her heartbeat to slow and her head to clear.

The image was still burned on her brain, and she sighed softly and savored it for a long moment. Then she firmly put it out of her mind.

AFTER THE EVENTS of the day, Thom assumed he'd fall into a deep sleep almost immediately. But every time he closed his eyes, his thoughts returned to the woman he'd invited into his home.

When he finally drifted off, images of Malin continued to tease at his mind. Then he awakened and realized that she was so close, close enough to call her name, close enough to find her and carry her into his bed.

Women had a very specific place in his life, a purely sexual place. He'd had a number of affairs over the years, but they'd never lasted long. Sooner or later, women realized that he never had any intention of truly opening himself up to them.

Something as simple as affection had never been present in his childhood, and he didn't find it necessary in his adult life, either. Pure desire didn't require romance to burn hot and intense.

Maybe Malin was right to keep their relationship on a platonic, businesslike level. He wasn't capable of romance, and she didn't strike him as the type who'd indulge in carnal pleasures without it. Hell, in his experience, no woman was truly happy to avoid romance in favor of simple physical pleasure.

Thom tossed aside the covers and grabbed a pair of sweatpants, tugging them up around his hips before wandering out to the kitchen. He found Malin curled up on the sofa.

He squatted down beside her and took the opportunity to study her face. He hadn't realized how much her emotions colored her expressions. In sleep, she looked like a teenager, young and fresh-faced, a light sprinkling of freckles visible across the bridge of her nose.

He felt the familiar pull, the need to possess her, to touch her and seduce her, to prove that the desire he felt was mutual, even though she'd already admitted it was. Thom reached out and took a strand of her pale hair, rubbing it between his fingers.

She stirred slightly and he quickly stood, retreating to the kitchen. He made a pot of coffee and put breakfast on the stove. As he waited, Thom observed her from a distance. They had a whole day ahead of them. How would it end? Would they share another kiss, or would she put a quick end to his fantasies?

When the coffee was done, he poured a mug for each of them, then carried the mugs back to the sofa. He sat down next to her and set the mug in front of her nose, hoping the smell might wake her up. But Malin was obviously a deep sleeper. He tried calling her name, shaking her shoulder, tickling the bottom of her feet and pulling her hair, but nothing seemed to rouse her.

Finally, impatient, Thom gently pinched her nose shut. A few seconds later, she jerked, then waved her hand in front of her face. Thom quickly sat back and picked up the coffee mugs, clutching them in his hands.

"You're awake," he said, holding out the hot coffee.

Malin rubbed at her eyes and slowly sat up. Her fingers immediately went to her hair, and she ran them through the tangles before grabbing the mug with a nervous smile. "What time is it?"

"Early. Seven-thirty."

"I fell asleep," she murmured.

"I expected to find you curled up in front of the door."

She smiled. "I'm not used to staying up that late. I'm usually in bed by ten."

"Not much of a party girl?"

"I used to be," she said with a wistful tone. "When I lived in New York, we went out all the time. But I don't really have a lot of friends here. Most of my old friends are married and have children."

"Same with me," he said with a shrug.

A long silence grew between them as she sipped at her coffee. "So…so what do you do about it? I mean, how do you deal when you're…lonely? You have family, right?"

Thom shook his head. "Sure. But we really don't see each other that often. My brothers come to the games now and then. And we get together over the holidays at my grandmother's place." Thom drew a deep breath. "It's better to be alone, I think. No complications."

"Sometimes complications are nice," she said softly.

He'd never been very comfortable expressing his deepest thoughts, and now was no exception. Thom wanted to try again, to make her understand. Somehow it seemed important that Malin knew exactly who he was. But he was afraid the more he talked, the more she'd start to think he was too damaged.

He quickly stood, rubbing his hands together. "So, I've made us breakfast. I don't know when you need to be at work, but—"

"I don't have to go to the office to work," Malin said. "I can work from anywhere that has internet. But

I do want to stop at home and grab a few things, like clothes and my toothbrush."

"And I need to get a workout in and some ice time."

"And we should talk about a plan of attack," Malin added.

"Why are you doing this for me?" he asked, meeting her gaze.

"I thought I explained. Because the fans love you. And you belong here in Minneapolis."

"Your father doesn't agree."

"He's stubborn and a complete control freak. But I believe I can change his mind as long as you behave yourself."

"And you're going to see that I do?"

Malin nodded. "I've got a lot of ideas."

"And you're sure that the only way to make this work is for you to live here? With me?"

She paused. "Yes, that would be advisable. At least until I can...you know."

"Trust me to be good?"

"Yes," she said, tipping her chin up and meeting his gaze. "I want to help you. I think I can."

She stood up, her body brushing against his. Their legs were caught between the coffee table and the sofa as both of them tried to avoid contact. Instead, their legs got tangled, and Malin began to lose her balance.

Thom grabbed her waist, but she was already falling backward onto the wide sofa. He landed on top of her, absorbing most of his weight with his arms. For a moment, neither one of them moved.

Their bodies seemed to fit together perfectly, as if

her every curve had been sculpted especially for him. Thom reached up and brushed a strand of hair out of her eyes. Their color in the low light of the morning was stunningly vivid, a pale blue.

"God, you are beautiful," he murmured.

"I bet you say that to all the girls," she teased.

Thom shook his head. "If I have, I'm sure I didn't mean it...until now."

It seemed the most natural thing to do next was to kiss her. He couldn't seem to keep himself from touching her. But he also wanted her to trust him.

"Since we'll be living together, perhaps we should try to defuse the...tension now," he suggested.

"You may be right," she breathed.

He moved slowly, giving her every chance to refuse. Nothing in her expression displayed a negative response. "Oh, hell, why not?" he muttered as he bent over her.

Thom brushed his lips against hers in a gentle test. She responded immediately. Her fingers slipped around his nape and a shiver raced through his body. Every nerve came alive and every sensation was magnified until he felt as if a simple touch could send him over the edge.

The kiss spun out like a spell around them, washing away any hesitation that either of them possessed. This was what he craved, yet until this very moment, he hadn't known it. There was a sweet warmth in her kiss and in the way her body responded to his.

She arched against him, pressing her soft curves against his muscle and bone. And whether it was just a temporary slip or something building between them, Thom didn't care. For now, he'd be satisfied to take anything she offered.

When he finally drew back, his gaze skimmed her perfect features. Her eyes fluttered open and she stared at him, wide-eyed and breathless. Her lips were damp and he stole one more kiss, sending her an apologetic smile.

Malin opened her mouth and he waited for a reprimand, but then she snapped it shut, her brow furrowing. Thom slowly got to his feet, then held his hand out for her. When she stood beside him, he distractedly smoothed her mussed hair and dragged his thumb across her lips. She tried to speak again, but he pressed his index finger against her mouth to stop her.

"All we were doing was defusing the tension. Now we can forget that happened. We don't have to talk about it. You don't have to be angry with me. We'll let that one go by." He started toward the kitchen. "I'll just get breakfast."

When he got to the kitchen, Thom opened the refrigerator and put his head inside, drawing a deep breath of the cold air. His head cleared, yet he couldn't forget what he'd just done. Why should he? It was obvious there was a powerful attraction between them. As much as Malin might want to deny it, that didn't change the fact it was there.

And why not act on it a bit more? Flirtation was a far cry from seduction. And Thom certainly had the self-control to stop before things got out of hand. He'd be the perfect gentleman.

"Can I help you with anything?" Malin stood at the kitchen island, her face flushed and her eyes bright.

"There's juice in the fridge," he said as he ladled oatmeal into two bowls. "And grab the blueberries from the freezer."

She fetched a few more items for him, then perched on a stool, watching him silently. He glanced over his shoulder, then cursed beneath his breath. "Do you want me to apologize? I will if you want me to. But I'm not sorry I kissed you. I enjoyed it and I think you did, too."

"I did," she said.

"Do you want me to promise it won't happen again? That would be another lie. It might happen. It might not. I prefer to leave my options open."

"I thought we were defusing the...tension," she said.

"It might need more defusing."

He set the oatmeal in front of her, sprinkled the blueberries on top, then squeezed honey over it all. She stared down at the bowl and grimaced.

"It's healthy," he said. "I eat it every day."

"It looks like wallpaper paste," she said.

"What do you usually eat for breakfast?"

"I usually grab a candy bar from the vending machine," she admitted.

He pulled the salmon from the oven and placed it on the counter. "Believe me, you'll enjoy this. And you won't be hungry again in twenty minutes."

"You eat fish for breakfast?" she asked.

"Or chicken. You have to have some protein, too." He chuckled. "You'd better enjoy it. It's the only thing I know how to cook."

Malin smiled and tasted the oatmeal. "It's good," she said. "Really. And I love salmon. I've just never eaten it for breakfast."

Thom slipped into the spot next to her and dug into his cereal. He'd always wondered what it might be like to have a woman in his life, eating meals together, enjoying their time together, even outside the bedroom. Thom had to admit that it was a pleasant experience, preparing a meal for her, chatting as they ate.

He hadn't seen the need for a personal assistant, but now that Malin was on board, he planned to enjoy every single moment.

"I'M REALLY NOT interested in having muscles." Malin stared at the barbell and shook her head. "When I agreed to work out with you, I was thinking of walking a little on the treadmill, maybe doing a few stretches, and that would be it."

Malin hadn't explored the second floor of the firehouse the night she arrived, but when Thom had decided to work out, she'd followed him upstairs to a huge room at the back of the building. The entire rear wall was windows, bathing the hardwood floors in sunshine. The brick walls were exposed and the room was filled with high-end exercise equipment.

Thom chuckled. "Oh, come on. Don't tell me you're one of those."

Malin felt warmth rise in her cheeks. "One of what?"

"A woman who doesn't sweat?"

"I—I sweat." She'd never claimed to be an athlete or even coordinated. Working out was not her favorite thing to do. Which was why she avoided it at all costs. "I do yoga. Two or three times a week."

"That's not exercise," he said. "That's posing in pretty outfits. You need to get your pulse up to burn calories," Thom said. "Start breathing harder."

"Oh, so kissing you is considered good cardio?" she shot back. Only after the words were out of her mouth did she realize she'd said them out loud. A quick change of subject was in order. "Do you think I'm fat?" she asked.

He held out his hand. "Hold on. Let's rewind to that first thing you said."

"No, answer my question. I can take it. There's absolutely nothing wrong with honesty." She looked down at her body, smoothing her hands over her hips. "Am I fat?"

He stared at her for a long moment, then shook his head. Slowly he approached her, his gaze locked on hers, a smile twitching at the corners of his mouth. "Are you fat? Hmm. Well, let me see. Turn around."

Malin groaned inwardly. Was he actually going to answer the question? Oh, God, if the kiss comment wasn't enough of a humiliation, now her physical imperfections were about to be pointed out in great detail. Well, she *had* said she could take it.

He stood behind her, and she waited for his verdict. But when she felt his hands slip around her waist, her breath caught in her throat. He splayed his fingers and then slid them down to her hips. A tiny gasp of surprise was all she could manage when he cupped her backside.

She slowly turned and faced him, her expression as calm as she could manage. "Well?"

"I haven't finished my examination," he teased. His hands found her waist again, but this time they moved up until his thumbs stopped at the curves of her breasts. Malin's pulse leaped and for a moment, she couldn't catch her breath. Would he touch her there?

"You're perfect," he said. "Perfect." With that, Thom walked away and grabbed a pair of dumbbells from the rack. He began to work on his biceps, watching his reflection in the mirror.

Malin walked over to the treadmill, glancing at him every now and then. She stepped onto the machine, her body still tingling from the aftereffects of his touch. It hadn't taken much to get her heart racing. Maybe if she exercised a bit, her body wouldn't react to him in such a disturbing way.

Who was she kidding? Wasn't this supposed to be how it went when you met an impossibly attractive man? Never mind the physical reactions. She was having more problems with her mind—the endless fantasies, the lack of coherent thought when he was in the room, the ability to relive every single moment of their last intimate encounter.

Maybe exercise could mitigate the physical problems, but she'd need to cut off her own head to take care of the rest. "Just focus," she muttered as she struggled to turn on the treadmill.

She punched the buttons and the display lit up, but the belt wasn't moving. Then she noticed the safety switch and pushed the plastic card into the slot. The treadmill yanked her backward, pulling her off balance.

Malin screamed as she was tossed off the treadmill, her arms flailing and her feet over her head. Before she hit the floor, she hit the corner of the weight bench. A searing pain on the crown of her head caused her to cry out again.

Thom was beside her in an instant. "Are you all right?"

Groaning, she pushed up on her elbow and touched her head gingerly. "I—I just slipped."

He stood up and switched off the treadmill. "You had it set for five miles an hour."

"Yeah? I guess that was my mistake." Her fingertips felt damp, and she looked at her hand to find her fingers dripping with blood. The room closed in on her, and Malin knew she was about to pass out. The sight of blood had always…been…her kryptonite…

She wasn't sure how long she was out, but when she opened her eyes, Thom was kneeling beside her, concern etched across his features.

"Hey there," he murmured.

He held her arm as she sat up, then pressed a damp towel to the back of her head. Malin winced. "Sorry. I always get a bit woozy at the sight of blood."

"Are you dizzy?"

"No," she said. "Just completely humiliated."

"Can you stand?"

"I—I'm not—"

He didn't give her a chance to try. Instead, Thom scooped her up in his arms and carried her down the stairs. Though she felt like a sack of potatoes, he carried her as if she barely weighed a thing. Malin closed her eyes and tried to appreciate the romance of the situation.

When they got to the living room, he didn't stop at the sofa. Instead, he carried her right into his bedroom and gently set her on the bed. "Stay there. Don't move."

Malin pulled the towel away from her head and was stunned at the amount of blood on the white terrycloth. She closed her eyes, fighting off another wave of dizziness but a few seconds later, Thom was back at her side.

He had a smaller washcloth and pressed it against the cut on her scalp. "I'm sorry to cause such a fuss," she said.

"You are a handful," he admitted.

"Has it stopped bleeding?"

"No. It'll probably need a few stitches." He glanced around the room, then reached for his cell phone sitting on the table beside the bed. After punching in a few numbers, he retreated to the hall to talk to whomever was on the line.

Malin tried to hear what he was saying, but in the end the effort was just too taxing. She snuggled down into the pillows, the cloth still pressed against the cut.

"Don't go to sleep!"

Malin opened her eyes. "I—I wasn't."

"If you have a concussion, you don't want to—"

"I don't have a concussion," she said. "I just cut myself."

"How hard did you bump your head? You did lose consciousness."

"From the sight of blood. Not from the injury," Malin explained.

"I called a doctor. Until he checks you out, I don't want you to sleep."

He crawled onto the bed and sat down behind her, taking over the care of her wound. "Scalp wounds always bleed a lot."

"I suppose you'd know. You've had your share of cuts over the years."

"I bet I've had more than two hundred stitches," he said.

Malin nodded. "I remember the cut you got last year, the one over your eye. That was pretty bad."

He gently grabbed her chin and turned her to meet his gaze. "You remember that?"

"Yeah," she said. "I was at that game. They took you in and stitched you up and you came back out and scored the game-winning goal. It was very impressive."

"You were watching me?"

"Every person in the place was watching you. Especially the women. They all love you. That's why I think it's important that you stay with the team. We have a lot of female fans. And they like bad boys."

He sighed, shaking his head. "Why is that? I mean, I've cultivated this reputation, and where has it gotten me? Maybe I ought to try being the good guy for once."

"Or maybe you should just be a little less bad," Malin said. She twisted her body until she faced him, determined to gauge his reaction to her suggestion. "I can help you with that. I can make you over into the kind of man that people admire. And not for fighting. You don't have to fight anymore. You're better than that."

"So you want to fix me," he asked.

"Not fix you," Malin said. "Just polish you up a bit. Would you let me do that?"

"I don't know," he said. "I'll have to think about it."

Malin nodded, then placed her palm on his cheek. For the first time since she'd met him, she saw a tiny hint of vulnerability in his expression. Would he trust her enough to let her in? Or would he fight her all the way?

The doorbell rang, the sound echoing through the interior of the fire station. "That's the doc," he said. "Hold on to the cloth. I'll go let him in."

Malin had to wonder how he'd gotten a doctor to make a house call, especially so quickly. But when the doctor strolled into the bedroom, she froze.

"Malin!"

"Drew?" She directed her gaze at Thom. "You called the team doctor?"

Drew strode into the room and set his bag on the floor beside the bed. "Let me take a look." Drew took the damp cloth from her hand and examined her wound.

"You shouldn't have called him," she said.

"Actually, he should have," Drew said. "He's right. You need stitches."

"I could have gone to the emergency room."

Drew chuckled. "And leave your wound to those hacks? I'm an expert at suturing. My work is infamous throughout the league." He reached into his bag and removed a syringe already filled with anesthetic. "This is going to pinch a bit, but it will pass."

Grudgingly she allowed Drew to tend to her, all the while holding her tongue. Malin's father had told her to watch Thom, but she was sure he hadn't intended for her to wind up in The Beast's bed. And if Drew said something to her father, the project and her ambitions would all be over before they'd even begun.

3

"IS THERE ANYTHING I can get for you?"

Thom smiled as he smoothed out the edge of his bedspread. Malin was exactly where he'd wanted her all along—in his bed. But the way she was looking at him didn't give him much hope that there would be seduction in their plans for the day.

"Why did you call Drew?"

"Who else should I have called?" Thom asked. "I had a woman in my apartment with a head wound. Some creative journalist could have turned that into an interesting story. Then add the fact that the woman was the team owner's only daughter and you've really got something juicy."

She hesitated for a moment. "What if Drew says something?"

"Do you really think he wants to be the one to spread a rumor about the owner's daughter and the team bad boy?"

"All right," she finally admitted. "You did the right thing. It was just a little uncomfortable."

"Why? Drew's a nice guy. Loyal to the team. Great doctor."

"He asked me out a couple months ago, and I told him I didn't date anyone I worked with. And then he walks in here and finds me in your bed. I'm still afraid he might say something."

Thom had never been the jealous sort, but her admission definitely brought out those feelings now. Maybe it was envy and not jealousy. "If you hadn't worked with him, would you have accepted?"

She shrugged. "Sure. He's a good-looking guy. And he's a doctor. Guys like him don't come around very often."

"Sure," he murmured. Thom turned away from the bed and walked into the bathroom. Drew was a doctor. College-educated. Exactly the kind of guy a woman like Malin needed. Dependable. Trustworthy. He was a goddamn doctor.

Thom stared at his reflection in the mirror. And what did he have to offer Malin? Nothing. He'd never gone to college. In a few years, the only job he'd ever had would cast him aside as too old and too slow. He'd be left with joints that barely worked and scars that would be constant reminders of the pain he'd endured. And if he was lucky, the money he'd invested would last long enough to make a comfortable life for himself. If he wasn't…he'd be as much of a failure as his father.

When he thought about his future, he'd always assumed he'd find a woman someday. But he'd imagined her as the puck bunny type, a girl who loved him for his fame as a hockey player and not for his prospects as a husband. But Malin was different. She'd never settle for less than the very best.

He raked his fingers through his hair, then examined the purple-and-yellow tinge of an old bruise above his eye. Maybe it was best to put any ideas of seduction out of his mind right now. After all, she was right to worry about Drew saying something. Thom was dangling by a very thin thread, and if anyone on the team found out that he'd kissed Malin, he'd be out the door in a heartbeat.

Malin had offered to help him, and he'd be grateful for her advice, but it had to stop there. Thom pushed away from the counter and walked back into the bedroom, a smile on his face. "Drew said you should spend the day resting. So just stay there and relax. Watch a little television, sleep, I'll get you something to eat and—"

"I can't stay here," she said. "This is your…bed."

"For now, it's your bed."

"There's nothing wrong with me. Drew said I probably didn't have a concussion."

"He also said to be safe, you shouldn't stress yourself today. Now, what would you like?"

"I'd love a cup of tea. With some honey."

"I think I can get you that."

Thom headed for the kitchen. To his surprise, he did have tea, left over from when he was last fighting a cold. He filled the teakettle and set it on the stove. Then he searched through the cupboards and freezer.

If she had to stay in bed all day, he'd have to make a trip to the store for more food.

The teakettle screamed, and he poured the water over the tea bag in the mug and carried it to her. Her attention was focused on her iPad. "Do you have a lot of work to do?"

"Some," she said as she took the tea. "Now that the season's over, most of the players are tweeting about their summer plans."

Most of the team had already scattered to their hometowns across the globe. His summer plans usually swung between time spent at his cabin on Mille Lacs Lake and completing renovation projects around the firehouse. But with his future in question, he wasn't sure what lay in store for him this summer.

"Do you want to sleep?"

"I think we should talk," Malin suggested. She patted the mattress beside her.

Thom circled the bed and sat down on the opposite side, stretching his legs out in front of him. "Is this all right? I'm not crowding you?"

Malin nodded. "I have some opportunities for you. The team won't be setting up any publicity events with you until a decision has been made about the trade. But that doesn't mean we can't get out there and shake up your image a bit."

"What is my image? Who am I supposed to be?"

"You could start by being friendly. More approachable. So we're going to do a little makeover."

"Oh, no," Thom said.

"Just a good haircut. And start shaving. The scruffy

look has to go, at least for the summer. And we're going to get you some decent clothes."

"I have plenty of clothes."

"Go to your closet," she said.

Thom did as ordered, standing in the doorway. "All right."

"Find me something that isn't gray or black."

"I like gray and black."

"When you dress like that, it makes you look… scary. Mean."

"I'm Tommy the Beast. I'm supposed to look mean."

"Not anymore. The Beast is dead," Malin said. "You're Thom Quinn, Nice Guy. The guy every girl wants to marry and every guy wants to call his friend."

"I sound like a real asshole," Thom muttered.

"I've made an appointment at a salon for tomorrow, and then a stylist friend of mine has agreed to see you. She'll have clothes for you to try on. After that, we just let you go."

"Let me go?"

"Yeah. You walk around the city, attend events, smile and pose for pictures. The pics show up on social media. We repost and retweet over and over. People say what a nice guy you are, how much they love you, and voilà! You become a different man."

"But that's not me," he said.

"It doesn't matter," Malin said. "Do you really think people know who you are now?"

Thom groaned as he stretched out on the bed, pulling a pillow over his head. "If I just stay here, maybe it will all just go away."

She slid down beside him and gently pulled the pillow back. "Try to stay positive about this," she said.

It was something his brother Tris would have said. He smiled at her, at the earnest expression on her face, at the notion that she could possibly turn him into a different man. Did she even realize the depth of the task she'd agreed to do? Thom reached out and cupped her cheek with his palm.

The moment he touched her, the impulse to take more was impossible to deny. He wanted to kiss her, to pull her slender body against his. Thom knew he should fight it, had just decided he wasn't going seduce her again. But the desire between them offered a comfort and clarity he hadn't known in far too long.

He slipped his arm around her waist and pulled her closer, so close that he could feel the warmth of her breath against his face. "We probably shouldn't do this," he whispered.

"I don't have a concussion," she said. "I'm in full possession of my faculties." She frowned. "That doesn't sound right. My facilities? Is that it?" Malin paused. "Maybe I do have a concussion."

He chuckled, dropping a quick kiss on her lips. "The doc said you don't have a concussion."

"So there's no reason we can't do this," she said.

"There are a million and one reasons," Thom countered.

"What if we can come up with one good reason to continue?" Malin asked.

"Oh, I can do that."

"All right, what is it?"

Thom wasn't used to talking about sex, and the idea of putting his desires into words was a bit intimidating. That was better left to poets and songwriters.

"Tell me," she whispered.

"Because it would be as close to perfect as I could ever hope to come," he said.

"You?"

"No, you," he said. "You're way out of my league, Ms. Pedersen."

Malin stared at him for a long moment, then pushed him back into the bed and crawled on top of him. Her legs straddled his waist, and she ran her palms over his chest. Thom held his breath, wondering where she planned to take this next.

She urged him to sit up, then reached for the hem of his T-shirt. When it was off, she tossed it across the room. Malin wasn't leaving any doubt about her intentions, because next she tugged her shirt off and threw it on top of his.

Thom had been with a lot of different women, but he couldn't remember ever feeling so nervous about the prospect of a full-on seduction. In the past, it had always been about pleasure and release, nothing beyond a physical attraction.

But from the moment he'd first seen Malin in that conference room, he'd been intrigued. Was it simply because an affair with her was dangerous? If anyone found out, it would most definitely end his career with the Blizzard. Or was there something more complicated at work?

She wore a lacy white bra beneath the loose top, and

he became fascinated by the delicate edge lying against the soft flesh of her breast. Thom wanted to take in the simple details of her skin, to appreciate the beauty of her body. For the first time, he wanted to slow down and enjoy every moment.

It took forever to get them both undressed, and yet he couldn't imagine it any other way. They were too curious about each revelation. Her slender body reacted to every one of his touches, and her pale skin was like silk beneath his fingertips.

When she was completely naked, he pressed her back onto the bed and let his gaze drift down her body. He traced a line with his finger from her bottom lip to her neck and then lower until he circled the hard pink tip of her nipple.

Malin moaned softly and arched her back. He bent over and drew her nipple into his mouth, teasing at it with his tongue until she twisted beneath him. Her fingers found the hard length of his shaft, and she wrapped them around him.

The sensation of pure pleasure nearly sent him over the edge, and he clenched his jaw to try to regain control. This had never happened to him before. But then, he'd always been very focused when it came to sex. With Malin, he had no idea what he was doing and where it was all leading.

"Are you sure about this?" he whispered. He drew back and looked down into her eyes.

She nodded, pulling him into a deep and passionate kiss. "Are you?"

Thom was ready to give her the quick answer. Hell,

he was always ready for sex. But he couldn't bring himself to say it. He might get only one chance with Malin. He didn't want to let it slip by so quickly. Instead he wanted to drag each step out. Yet the expectations were there. She'd probably heard all the rumors about his womanizing. Maybe she expected him to be some kind of sex god. And while the doctor had said she was fine to go about her regular activities, Thom was sure the doc hadn't had this in mind. When they finally made love—as Thom was sure they would— he wanted it to be when he could take them both to the very limits of pleasure and beyond.

"I think we should stop," Thom said.

"Stop? But why?"

"Drew told you to take it easy today. And the two of us together might…well, it might be too much for you to handle. After all, you do have a head wound."

"We're already naked," she said.

"We could still enjoy that. Maybe you could show me your tattoos? I could give you a tour of my hockey scars."

"I don't have any tattoos," Malin said.

He rolled off her and grabbed a felt-tip pen from the bedside table. "I could give you one," Thom said. "What would you like? And where would you like it?"

She seemed puzzled at first, as if the sudden change in direction were the very last thing she expected. "Let me think about it," Malin murmured. "Why don't you start with your hockey scars?" She sat up and pulled the blankets over her lap, then brushed her tangled hair away from her face. "Go ahead. Begin."

He crawled out of bed and pulled her up to her feet, then walked her over to the full-length mirror on the back of the door. As he stood there, looking at them both in their natural state, Thom was aware of one very simple notion.

This was the woman he'd been waiting for. And until this very moment, he hadn't even known he'd been waiting.

IT WAS, QUITE POSSIBLY, the strangest day that Malin had ever spent with a man in her life. From the moment it had all begun, she'd thought that they'd toss aside all their inhibitions and indulge in wild, frantic sex. She'd been ready for it. In truth, she'd convinced herself that it was the only option.

But then they'd started talking and couldn't seem to stop. The vulnerability of the two of them, curled up on his bed, completely naked and ready to surrender, seemed to open them to some crazy kind of confessional.

He'd told her that he'd started stealing to feed his family. That on his first day of juvie, he'd been so scared he'd cried himself to sleep. And that every time he laced up for a game, he was still worried someone would say it had all been a mistake and he didn't deserve the chances he'd been given.

Malin had confessed that she felt like that, too, only in her nightmares it was her father telling her she wasn't good enough. Would never be good enough.

Eventually there was a lull in their conversation and Malin grabbed her iPad. "I know what we should do,"

Malin said. "We need to make you a Twitter account. And one for Instagram, too."

"No," Thom said. "I don't want to deal with all that."

"You don't have to. I will. I do it for a bunch of the other guys. If they don't send me something, I just make something up and post it. It's always something positive, so it's a good thing."

"What difference would it make?" Thom asked.

"You'd be surprised," Malin said. "It's the best way to communicate with your fans. Jeff Stromhall has almost a million followers. And he can talk to each and every one of them just by typing in a short little message every day."

Thom rolled over and peered down at the screen of Malin's iPad. "Show me how it works," he said.

Malin quickly prepared a Twitter page for him, copying photos from the Blizzard site and answering bio questions for him. "Here's your name. Thomquinn3. And your picture from the team site. And here's your banner picture—the overtime goal that you scored against Chicago."

"Nice," he said.

"All right, now you have to say something. It should be short and pithy. You only have one hundred forty characters."

"Pithy," he said. "I'm not sure I've ever said anything pithy."

"Then something inspiring. Or interesting. Or witty."

Thom groaned and ran his fingers through his hair. "This is a lot of pressure. I don't want to sound stupid."

"Anything."

He flopped back into the pillows and covered his eyes with his arm. Malin watched him, surprised that a guy unafraid to start a brawl on the ice was so scared to say something about himself.

"All right," he said. "How about this? 'Nothing better than a lazy afternoon—'"

Malin held up her hand to stop him while she typed in the first part of the message. She nodded for him to continue.

"'In bed with a very beautiful and very naked woman.'"

Malin stopped typing and looked up at him. "You can't say that."

"But it's true."

"Some things should be kept private."

"All right, you make something up.'

"Fine. How about, 'Lazy afternoon watching my favorite movie.' What's your favorite movie?"

"The Wizard of Oz."

"You like *The Wizard of Oz*?" Malin shook her head. She really knew nothing about this man at all. "Tommy the Beast's favorite movie is *The Wizard of Oz*."

"I like the flying monkeys. And the lion. And the Munchkins. It's been my favorite movie since I was a little kid. What's wrong with it?"

Malin smiled. "Nothing. It's perfect." She keyed in the tweet. "'Lazy afternoon watching my favorite movie, The Wizard of Oz. There's no place like home.'" She showed it to him and he nodded. "Click Send," she urged him.

He sent the tweet. "All right, I'll go get the DVD. I haven't watched it in years. We always used to watch it around Christmas."

"We haven't talked much about your family," Malin said. Beyond what he'd said about why he'd started stealing, Thom had avoided mentioning his family. He'd mentioned his two brothers, Tristan and James. From what she'd made out, his parents hadn't played much of a role in raising them, but his grandmother had.

"I don't want to tell you more sad stories," he said. "That's all part of the past."

"It's part of who you are," she said.

Thom shook his head. "No, it's not." He turned away, his gaze fixed on a stream of sunshine coming through the bedroom curtains. "Yes, it is. You're right. But some of it is just so...pitiful. I never wanted people to pity me. I think that's why I was okay with the whole Tommy the Beast image. My past made me tough. Not...wounded."

"Are you wounded?" Malin tried to keep the tremor out of her voice, but it was nearly impossible. Just looking at his expression, tinged with torment, brought forth a surge of emotion. She didn't want to cry. It would only confirm the worst of his fears.

"My father died when I was a kid. I've been told that he was a great guy—funny, the life of the party. My parents were just eighteen when they got married, and they were happy until my father lost his job. He started drinking a lot and my mum had to work longer hours. She worked nights so that they didn't have to pay for child care, although my da wasn't around much once my older brother, Tristan, was able to watch over us. I was about ten when the bad times started."

"Did he get sick?"

"My father was killed trying to rob a gas station. My mother started drinking after he left, and things got even worse when they sent us into the foster care system. We bounced in and out of that, back and forth between my mother and the system. There was the occasional nice family and some not-so-nice group homes. Sometimes we were together, sometimes not. We rarely had money and we lived out of our car one summer. School was a joke. But then one of my foster parents enrolled me in an after-school hockey program. I learned to skate and play the game, and I was good at it." He'd avoided her gaze for most of his story, but he took a moment to look at her. "Do you feel sorry for me?"

Malin shook her head. She crawled closer to him and tucked herself beneath his arm, then pulled him down to lie next to her. Their naked limbs tangled beneath the bed linens, and she pressed a kiss to the center of his chest. "Did your brothers play hockey?" she asked, hoping she'd found a question that might keep him talking.

"No, they had their own interests." A long silence descended between them. He grabbed her hand and began to toy with her fingers, weaving them through his as he contemplated his next words. "So, do you pity me?"

"No, I really like you. I mean, really, really, I do. I never expected to like you so much."

"I like you, too," he murmured.

Thom slipped his hand around her waist and pulled her naked body against his. The contact was electric, and Malin felt the breath suddenly leave her body. When he wanted something, Thom Quinn didn't hesitate to take it.

He kissed her and she was lost in the sweet taste of his mouth, the way he drew away and toyed with her bottom lip, catching it between his teeth before kissing her again.

Thom rolled over her, stretching his body out over the length of hers. Malin loved the weight of his flesh pressing against her breasts and hips.

"Do you know what I think we should do?" he asked.

Malin swallowed hard, wondering if this was when they'd finally make love. She was ready. She'd even considered taking control herself but then remembered he had his own reasons for the delay.

"We should go on a date," he continued. "I'm going to take you to dinner. I know this wonderful Italian place right in the neighborhood. They have the best lasagna. If you hate lasagna, they have—"

"We can't go out," Malin said. "If I'm seen with you, there'll be photographs and all kinds of speculation."

"I'm not always recognized," he said.

"All it takes is one photo to be posted online and suddenly you and I are engaged. Believe me, I know how these things can flare out of control."

"I guess you're right," he murmured.

"We could always call and get takeout."

He nodded, but Malin saw the disappointment in his eyes. She should have been pleased about the prospect of a real date, but in truth, she had to be realistic.

If he was traded, they would never see each other again. And if he wasn't, there was no way she could continue to sleep with him. As soon as his fate was decided, hers would be, too. Thom Quinn would be off-limits.

SHE SLEPT CURLED against his body, her legs tucked into his lap, her chin resting on his shoulder. Thom couldn't remember the last time he'd felt so absolutely content with his life. As long as she was with him, all was well with the world.

Still, he knew it was only a matter of time before the wolves were at the door. He'd never regretted the choices he'd made in his life until this very moment. And now all the stupid moves had come back to haunt him. The drinking and the women and the partying had poisoned the possibility of a happy future.

Though he knew a relationship with Malin was impossible, he couldn't make himself stop dreaming that it could be. He imagined the two of them together, living a normal life, finding happiness in the simple things they shared. She was the first woman he'd ever met who seemed to understand and accept him—the good and the bad.

But if life had taught him anything, it had taught him that wishes and dreams were a waste of time. Happiness was for other people, not him. But Malin was with him now, and he was determined to enjoy it for as long as it lasted.

He rolled over onto his back and felt something hard pressing into his hip. Thom pulled out Malin's tablet. Curious, he turned it on. The Twitter page she had made for him came up, and he skimmed the heading. "Two thousand seven hundred and three followers," he murmured. What did that mean?

He leaned over and gave Malin a gentle shake. "Malin," he whispered. "Wake up."

She moaned, burrowing deeper into the bedcovers. But when he shook her again, she opened her eyes and gazed up at him. "What time is it?"

"Early. About four a.m."

"Too early," she murmured.

He held out the tablet. "Look at this. I have followers. What does that mean?"

"That's good," she said. "People are finding your account and signing up to see what you have to say. Almost three thousand—that's a lot of people for such a short time. And once we link you to the team page, you'll probably have a half million within a week."

Thom wasn't sure what that all meant, but as long as Malin was happy, then so was he. He dropped the tablet on the bed and curled up against her. "Are you awake?"

"I am now," she said.

"I was thinking we could still have that date we were talking about."

"We discussed that," Malin said.

"There's somewhere I want to take you. For breakfast. And I promise, no one will know we're there."

She turned over to face him. "At four a.m.? You want to have a date right now."

"Yeah."

She smiled. "All right. I suppose you're not going to let me get any more sleep." She sat up and ran her fingers through her tangled hair. "What do I need to wear?"

"This place is very casual," he said. "It might be a bit chilly outside, though, so wear a sweater."

Malin nodded, watching him from the bed, the covers pulled up around her bare breasts. Though they'd spent an entire day naked, the idea of watching her dress suddenly seemed awkward. Thom grabbed his clothes from the floor and headed to the bathroom.

He closed the door behind him, then quickly brushed his teeth and ran a comb through his hair. As he tested his jawline with the back of his hand, he decided on a quick shave. Who knew what might transpire later in the day? The last thing he wanted was to hurt her delicate skin with a beard burn.

When he emerged from the bathroom, she was waiting, sitting on the edge of the bed, fully dressed with her hands resting in her lap. Thom held his hand out and pulled her to her feet. "You look beautiful."

She frowned, shaking her head. "I'm wearing the same clothes I was wearing yesterday."

"That doesn't change the fact that you're beautiful."

He tucked her hand in his, and they walked out of the firehouse and onto the eerily quiet street. "I've never been out this late," Malin said, quickening her pace to keep up with Thom's stride.

Though they could have driven, the breakfast place was just four blocks from his home. Thom's downtown neighborhood was a mix of commercial properties, parking lots and old warehouses and factories that had been turned into residential lofts.

The streets were dark and silent, so quiet that their footsteps echoed against the brick buildings. "It's kind of spooky out here," she said.

He pulled her hand up to his lips and gave it a kiss. "You're perfectly safe," he assured her. "You're with The Beast."

EXCEPT TO MALIN, he didn't feel like a beast at all. In truth, Thom Quinn was nothing like Tommy the Beast. He was quiet and soft-spoken, a bit unsure of himself, nothing at all resembling his on-ice persona. She hadn't expected to respect him so much.

He led her into a narrow alleyway, and Malin frowned. The scent of baked goods suddenly filled the air, and Thom grinned. "Smell that?"

"Yes! What kind of place is this?"

He climbed a short flight of steps and held open a screen door. "It's called Doughnut Nirvana. A friend of mine owns it. They make fifty varieties of dough-nuts every day."

They walked directly into the kitchen, which was blazing with light and activity. Everyone greeted Thom by name and he returned the greetings, knowing each of the workers personally. A woman wearing a black baseball cap hurried toward them and pulled Thom into a fierce hug.

"Malin, this is Nora. She owns this place."

Malin held out her hand, but Nora ignored the gesture and pulled her into a hug. "Nice to meet you. So nice," she said. "Tommy's never brought a girlfriend with him."

"Oh, I'm not his—"

"Well, you must be someone special. He's never even brought a guest before." Nora drew her along to a small table set in a quiet corner of the kitchen. A few seconds later, Thom joined them with a couple of mugs filled with steaming coffee.

He sat down across from her. "Get ready to be amazed," he said.

Before she could ask why, one of the bakers appeared with a plate heaped with freshly made doughnuts. "I have very few weaknesses," Malin admitted, "but kind men and freshly made pastries are at the top of the list. Are these all for us?"

"Nora calls this her tasting menu. She expects us to taste each one and give her feedback."

Malin giggled. "This *is* nirvana."

"I thought you might like it," he said.

"How did you know?"

"Try this one." He held up a long rectangular doughnut with a strip of crispy bacon laid on top of what smelled like maple frosting.

Malin took a bite and rolled her eyes. "So good." She took another bite, then a sip of her coffee.

As Thom had promised, the doughnuts kept coming, all with imaginative flavor combinations, beautifully frosted and still slightly warm. It was the most perfect breakfast she'd ever eaten.

"We have to take some pictures for Twitter," Malin said.

"Who's going to care what I eat for breakfast?" he asked.

"All your followers," she said. "And it won't be just to inform them of what you ate. You're also going to plug the bakery. You just watch. She'll have a line out the door by next week."

"How is that possible?"

Malin lined the plates up in front of him, then held up her phone to take a photo. "Smile," she said. She took one picture, then told him to give her a thumbs-up for the next. "Now pick up that chocolate doughnut and take a big bite out of it." She snapped one last photo, then showed Thom the results. "I like the thumbs-up best."

"Me, too," Thom said.

"Now we have to compose the tweet. How about, 'Breakfast of champions. Doughnut Nirvana. Hashtag off-season.'"

"Hashtag?"

"It's just a little thing you add for humor. We wouldn't want anyone to think you eat like this during the season."

"And now you post it?"

"Not yet. We'll do it after we leave or else there'll be a swarm of people here trying to get your autograph."

Malin laughed. "Oh, look, you have another five hundred followers."

He shook his head. "Are you sure we ought to let the team know I eat doughnuts for breakfast?"

Malin smiled. He was starting to think strategically. "It's all in good fun. And it helps you appear a bit more approachable." Malin plucked a strawberry-filled doughnut off the plate. "When did you meet Nora?"

"We were in foster care together. She came to me when she wanted to start the bakery, and I bought the building for her. As long as she's paying me back, I get free doughnuts."

"That was nice of you," Malin said. "And it's a wonderful story. People should hear it."

"No, it's just something I did for Nora. There wasn't a bank in the city who'd lend her money. She had a criminal record and they said she was too much of a risk. But she proved them wrong, and the bakery is doing really well. Nora is happy."

"If you want to vanquish The Beast, people are going to need to see the softer side of you."

"I don't like to expose that side," he said. "It's usually easier to be The Beast."

Malin felt a surge of frustration. There were moments when Thom was ready to shed the old image, to toss it off like an armor he no longer needed. But then he'd draw it back on again, ready for the next battle. Would she ever be able to get him to shed it completely? Maybe not, but Malin was determined she'd at least shine it up a bit.

They nibbled at the rest of the doughnuts and gave

Nora a list of their personal favorites. Malin took a few more pictures with the owner, then warned her that there might be a sudden influx of customers over the next week.

As they walked out of the shop into the early morning light, she showed Thom how to post the tweet and then pulled up the picture. He slipped his arm around her shoulders and pulled her close, pressing a kiss to the top of her head.

"Your stitches look good," he said.

"I need to take a shower and wash my hair," she murmured. "And then we have that appointment at the salon."

"You're not going to do something weird with my hair, are you?"

"Like what?"

"I don't know. Dye it or give it some of those bleached highlights."

"No. Just a cut. And while we're at it, I'd recommend some decent shaving products and a good razor. And a skin care regimen. And a manicure and pedicure might be nice."

"Oh, no," he warned. "I'm not getting my nails painted."

"They don't do that for men. And don't write it off so quickly. I think you'd enjoy it."

When they got home, Malin checked her tablet again. To Thom's surprise, he had comments on his photo from the bakery. "Here's one," she said. "This is from Twin City Tribes. They're kind of a sports gossip site. They have about a million followers. Look, they've commented on your picture. 'Bad boy Tommy Quinn has breakfast with—'" Malin stopped short, then shook her head. "Oh, hell."

"What?" Thom asked, sitting down beside her on the sofa.

"'Bad boy Tommy Quinn has breakfast with mystery blonde,'" she said.

"How did they know you were there? You're not in the picture."

Malin tapped the screen a few times, then pointed to a stainless steel napkin holder on the table. "And there I am. My reflection, clear as day."

"I wouldn't say that was clear as day. You can't really tell who it is."

"You can tell it's a woman," Malin said. She stood up and began pacing. "I know better than this. Always check the photo. Enlarge it. Examine every square inch."

"Can't we just delete it?" Thom asked.

"No, that would only call more attention to it," Malin said. "We just have to let it play out."

"I can just post another message saying you're just a friend."

"No, you don't engage in conversations or arguments with your followers. Rule number one."

"I thought rule number one was check the photos carefully."

"What if my father sees this?" Malin said. She shook her head. "What am I talking about? I'm the one who usually shows him this stuff. He'd never look at it on his own." She sighed. "We should be safe. We'll just need to be more careful."

"Give me that thing," Thom said, grabbing her tablet from her hands. "Delete it right now. The whole thing. This is just too much pressure."

"No, it will be fine," Malin said. "We'll post a picture of your new haircut this afternoon, and the mysterious blonde will be forgotten in no time."

Thom wrapped his arm around her neck and pulled her into a fierce hug. "You're the boss, boss. But, just so you know, I have no intention of forgetting the mysterious blonde."

4

"I WANT YOU to open your mind to new experiences," Malin said as she pulled into the alley behind the salon and day spa. "Forget about what men are supposed to look like and just enjoy yourself."

"They're going to cut my hair," Thom said. "I think I can handle that. Just as long as they don't put all that crap in my hair after they're done. What do they call that stuff? Product. No product."

"Open mind," she repeated.

"So I'm just supposed to let you have your way with me?"

"I let you have your way with me," she said, glancing over at him as she brought her car to a stop. "Fair is fair."

"So, if I do what you say this afternoon, you'll do what I say tonight?"

"Don't push your luck," Malin said.

"I always do."

She got out of the car and waited for him at the back

door of the salon. She'd arranged for the full slate of beauty services for him, but she'd decided to hold off on telling him the rest of the plan until she was sure he could handle a makeover.

Malin's friend Amy met them at the back door and brought them into a private area in the rear of the salon, which was set up for clients who preferred a purely private experience. Amy brought them over to a sofa and handed both Malin and Thom a spa menu. "What can we do for you today?" she asked.

"I'm here for a haircut," Thom said, holding the menu out to her. "Just a basic one."

Amy's eyebrow shot up. "You don't want to have a little fun? Wait right here."

"What does she mean by *fun*?" Thom asked.

"Why don't you pamper yourself? Have a massage or a facial. You definitely need a pedicure. And as long as they're working on your feet, they can do your hands. Your nails are a mess."

"I'm a guy," Thom said. "I'm supposed to be a mess."

"But we're working on a new you. A more *together* you. It's important to look the part."

"No one is going to see my feet."

"It's summer. You don't wear flip flops?"

Amy reappeared with a tray holding two champagne flutes and a carafe of mimosa. She poured a glass for each of them and smiled. "Now, what's up first?"

Thom downed the first mimosa, then refilled it and downed a second. "You're in charge," he said to Malin.

She smiled. She'd expected him to put up more of a

fight, and she was happy that he trusted her enough to go with her plans. Though she had to wonder what he'd try to take in return. A tiny shiver skittered through her body at the thought of them back in the privacy of his bedroom, and her mind began to form her own menu.

"Let's start with a manicure and pedicure," she said. "Then we'll do a facial and a shave and finish off with a haircut and style. And if he isn't crazy by then, we'll consider a massage at the end."

"How long are we staying?" Thom asked.

"As long as it takes to get the last of the beast out of you," Malin said.

"I thought we were seeing some stylist, too."

"If we can fit it in, absolutely."

"Changing rooms are back there," Amy said. "Grab a men's robe and get comfortable."

Thom grinned and stood, then held out his hand to Malin. She glanced over at Amy, a blush warming her cheeks. "You don't need me to help you change," she murmured.

"If I'm going through all this, you're going to do it with me. Come on. Let's get you into a fancy robe."

Reluctantly Malin followed Thom to the changing rooms. She hadn't planned to indulge herself today, but if it made things easier with Thom, then all the better. Once he found out where they were headed after their morning at the spa, he might not feel as pleased with her.

She reached for the door of the changing room and slipped inside. But at the last moment, Thom followed her, leaning back against the door to close it. He reached for the hem of his T-shirt and pulled it over his head, then tossed it on a nearby chair.

"What are you doing?" she murmured, her gaze fixed on his muscular torso.

"Changing," he said. "Am I supposed to be completely naked under the robe?"

Malin swallowed hard. "No, no. You can leave your underwear on."

He kicked off his trainers, then unzipped his cargo shorts and let them drop at his feet. Though she'd seen him naked earlier that morning, she'd forgotten the effect his body had on her senses. Malin fought the impulse to reach out and hook her finger in the waistband of his boxer briefs to draw him closer.

"Do you need some help?" he asked, his eyebrow arched.

"With?"

"Removing your clothes?"

She drew in a sharp breath and shook her head. "No, I'm fine." Malin grabbed a men's robe from the stack and shoved it at his chest. "Why don't you just go ahead and get started. I'll be along in a minute."

Thom grinned and wrapped his hands around her waist. "I'm thinking this could be fun. It sure as hell is something I've never done before. And it's nice, just the two of us, together."

He pressed her back against the wall of the changing room and pinning her hands beside her head. Then he kissed her roughly. His body slid up against hers, and she could feel his shaft growing hard with every moment that passed.

It was difficult to remember that they hadn't yet made love. In truth, they hadn't done much more than kiss and touch each other. And yet they were completely comfortable shedding their clothes—at least, he was.

But she had to remember that they were in a public place, and both of their reputations were on the line.

"We can't do this," she murmured as he caught her bottom lip between his teeth. "Go."

"I think you'd better go first," he said with a low chuckle. "I need to calm down."

She glanced down to his erection straining at the fabric of his briefs. "Look at what you've done!"

"Me? You're the one to blame for that."

Malin quickly stripped out of her clothes and tugged on a robe, then opened the door. "You stay right here until that—" she waved her hand in the direction of his crotch "—that…problem is gone."

Of course, Thom didn't do as he was told. Instead he shoved his hands in the robe pockets and held the thick fabric over his lap as he walked out, hiding his desire from anyone who might suspect.

Two young women waited at the pedicure chairs, but Thom held back, his expression perplexed. Deciding to lead by example, Malin crawled up onto the chair. She stuck her feet into the deep basin of hot water and sank back into the massage cushions. Finally he joined her, careful to tuck his robe shut over his lap.

"I'm sitting on a throne," he muttered.

Malin handed him the massage controls. "Put your feet in the tub," she said.

"What's in the water?"

"Schools of piranhas," she teased. "They'll nibble at your feet until they're all smooth and pretty."

Thom looked down at the aesthetician, and she shook her head. "It's just soap and essential oils."

"Great," Thom muttered. He snatched up a magazine from the rack beside him and opened it, then glanced at the cover. "I guess they don't have *Sports Illustrated*?"

Amy appeared with a stack of reading material that included both sports-and-fitness and fashion titles. "Happy?" Malin asked.

"I'm in a state of bliss," he said, his voice dripping with sarcasm.

Malin giggled. Though he protested, he did as he was told and, after a few moments, seemed to relax. Once again, Thom had surprised her. She'd assumed he'd be his usual beastly self with the public. Then again, every time she thought she knew how he'd respond, he found a way to surprise her.

Malin had often wondered what kind of man it would take to captivate her for an entire lifetime. The notion of finding a mate who could keep her interest for fifty or sixty years seemed like an impossibility. And there were so many different qualities she sought in a man—humor, kindness, loyalty, wit, intelligence…so many qualities that she'd convinced herself she'd never find her perfect match.

And yet here she was, with a hockey player burdened by a huge chip on his shoulder. A man who'd describe himself as self-destructive. A man who'd probably never had a normal relationship with a woman in his life. But beneath the grit and grime that he used as a shield, there was a very special man.

"You're right," he murmured.

She turned her head to find him smiling at her. "I am? About what?"

"My feet were hideous."

"I never said that. I just recommended the pedicure."

"They were hideous. But look at them now." He pulled a foot out of the water. "All pretty and soft."

"Kissable," she said.

"Yeah?"

"Mmm-hmm."

"Well, that would be something new."

She leaned back in her chair and closed her eyes, a smile curling the corners of her mouth. After all the women he'd been with, Malin had wondered if there was any sexual territory he'd left unexplored. And now she knew there was. "You're telling me that you've never had your toes sucked?" she asked.

"I've never been much of a foot person," he said. "Giving or receiving."

She sighed and shook her head. "So much you've missed out on. I guess you'll just have to be educated."

He reached out and took her hand, pulling it to his lips. Then Thom drew the tip of her little finger into his mouth and gently sucked. "I've always been an excellent student."

With a quick glance at the spa attendants, Malin snatched her hand away.

THOM HAD NEVER had to work too hard at wooing women. They always seemed to just appear in his life when he wanted them, ready to accept whatever he was prepared to give them. Sometimes, that was nothing more than a night in bed. Other times, a vacation. But it never lasted more than a week or two.

But later that afternoon, he found himself in a designer suit, silk tie and finely pressed shirt. Though a suit was standard wardrobe for travel to and from every hockey game, the clothes in Thom's closet didn't sport any designer labels. Many of his teammates spent their money on tailored suits and Italian shoes, but Thom had never put any value on such overpriced affectations. Expensive clothes didn't make him a better hockey player or a better man, so what purpose did they serve? They were a waste of money.

He glanced over at Malin. She was peering at a computer monitor, quietly discussing the last round of photos they'd taken with her stylist friend. They'd been stuffing him into various monkey suits for almost three hours, and his patience was beginning to wear thin. At the spa, she'd refused even to touch him, and since they'd arrived at the stylist's, he might as well have been a mannequin for how brusquely Malin treated him.

Though she'd explained that her friend, a local menswear designer, needed a celebrity model for some fancy magazine shoot, he hadn't expected to be dressed and undressed like a freaking doll for the entire afternoon.

Cursing beneath his breath, Thom loosened the tie

and unbuttoned the top button of his shirt as he walked away from the backdrop. "I'm done," he said.

He strode back to the dressing room where he'd left his regular clothes, anxious to shrug back into a skin that felt comfortable. Malin followed after him, her heels clicking on the tile floor of the photo studio.

"Thom, we just have one more look. I know this is a lot of hurry-up-and-wait, but I promise you that it will be worth it."

He rounded on her and she stopped short, nearly crashing into his chest. "Why are you doing this?"

"Because we can use these photos for your social media. So people can see you in a different light."

"People? Or you?"

"Me?"

"If you don't like the man I am, I'm not going to change just because I put on a fancy suit and shiny shoes."

"This isn't about me," Malin said.

"Isn't it? I think you'd like to see me as a man your father would respect. All these plans to fix me up have nothing to do with my job. I'm still going to get traded and have to leave my family. But you'll get what you want."

She stared at him, her mouth agape, then shook her head. "Take the suit off. We're done. I'll make our excuses to Francesca. We can leave as soon as you're dressed."

She stalked out of the dressing room, slamming the door behind her. Thom closed his eyes. He knew she was hurt and disappointed, and surprisingly it killed him that he was the cause of that. But she couldn't just order him around like some compliant little puppy. What would be next? It was better to remind her that he'd never change, before her expectations got completely out of hand.

He reached up to pull off the tie, then stopped himself. He'd never been a quitter. And it wasn't as if this photo shoot was physically taxing. All he had to do was stand around and look "natural." Though how that was possible wearing some of these clothes, he wasn't sure. Plus, he did like Malin's friend, and he wanted to help her career.

Thom rebuttoned his collar and fixed his tie, then headed back out into the studio. But as soon as he finished this photo shoot, he and Malin were going to have a serious talk about her plans to remake his image.

Everyone turned as he walked back into the studio, silently watching him as he retook his place. "Sorry about that," he murmured. "What do you need me to do?"

"I think we're done with this look," Francesca said. "Why don't we move on to the last one and we'll try to get you out of here quickly."

"No worries," Thom said. "I've got all the time in the world."

Malin walked to the rack of clothes, and Francesca handed her a cluster of hangers. Malin headed for the dressing room, not even glancing his way. He found her there, her attention fixed on straightening the laces on a pair of black sneakers.

"What's next?" he asked.

"These pants and this shirt," she said. She held up a box. "And these shoes with no socks. Francesca wants to redo your hair, so don't freak out."

"I didn't freak out," he muttered. "I'm just tired of standing around doing nothing."

"This process takes time. The photos could be blown up to billboard size. We want them to be perfect."

"Right," he said.

Malin forced a smile. "Thank you for doing this for me. Once we're done with this look, we can leave." She hurried out of the room.

Thom did his best to give the photographer a few good shots over the next half hour. He couldn't help but notice that Malin kept to the shadows, just out of sight, and did her best to avoid his gaze.

He was sorry he'd hurt her, but the idea that he and Malin where actually involved in a relationship was ridiculous. And if they'd didn't have a relationship, why did he even care what she thought?

Over the past few days, he'd been caught up in some silly fantasy that they might have something special, that he'd finally met a woman who could accept him for who he really was. But today was ultimate proof that she wanted someone very different.

They didn't speak to each other again until they were in the car, ready to leave the studio for his place. They'd brought her car, and when he slid into the passenger seat, she reached for the ignition, then paused.

"I'm sorry," she murmured. "I shouldn't have been so pushy. But I really am doing this for you."

"How do you figure?" he asked.

"I'm trying to find a way to get you noticed on social media in a positive way." She pulled out her phone and held it out. "Look, we posted a picture of your new haircut and you got a thousand likes and seventy-six retweets."

"What does that mean?"

"People are seeing the new you and—and they want to engage with you. They're interested." She pulled the phone away and tucked it back in her pocket. "We need them to be interested if we want to stop the trade."

"I just get the feeling that all of this is some big scheme to change who I am."

"Well, yeah, maybe it is," Malin said. "The women, the fights, the drinking. Don't you think you need to change?"

"It's a little late for that," Thom replied.

"No," she said. "I don't believe that."

"But it's not all some altruistic effort to make me into a better man. You want to prove a point to your father, and you want to use me to do it."

She reached for the key and started the car. He couldn't tell if she'd discarded his last accusation or if she was considering it in silence. For a long time as she drove, Malin didn't speak. Then she took a ragged breath. "Maybe you're right."

Thom cursed beneath his breath. Hell, he didn't want to be right. He risked a glance over at her, and he saw a tear trickle from the corner of her eye. It felt like a knife to his heart, and he wanted to take back all his doubts and anger. But he'd protected himself for such a long time by taking the other person down first, and the instinct was too hard to fight.

When they reached the firehouse, Malin parked her car out front but left it running. "I have some things I need to take care of at the office. I'll be back later."

"You're going to leave me alone?" Thom asked. "Are you sure that's wise?"

He didn't want her to go. Even though he was angry, he still wanted to keep her close. It was inevitable that that they'd argue, but he wasn't prepared to deal with the consequences.

"I guess I'll have to trust you."

"Don't," he warned. "I'm the last guy in the world you should trust."

Sighing deeply, Malin turned off the car then faced him. "Why do you want an argument? I'm not even sure what we're fighting about."

Just the fact that she could read him so well fueled his temper. Thom got out of the car and slammed the door behind him. He didn't want to care for her. Why couldn't she be like the other women he'd known— easy to bed and even easier to leave?

"I'm trying to help you," she shouted as she got out of the car and circled around to him. "You could show a little appreciation instead of acting like a petulant child."

"Or are you trying to fix me?" he asked.

"Wouldn't that be part of helping you? What was so bad about today? You got a nice haircut and some fashionable clothes—for free, I might add. Ideally, when you go out now, people will look at you differently."

She met his gaze, and Thom felt as if she could see directly into his soul. "It's time to grow up, Thom. Time to stop making the same mistakes over and over."

With that, she turned and walked to the front door of the firehouse. She waited for Thom to unlock it and when he did, she went inside, leaving him standing on the stoop.

Of course she was right about it all. Until she'd appeared, his life had been a mess. And now she was trying to help him, and his instinct was to fight against any authority.

Thom sat down on the stoop and raked his fingers through his new haircut. The stylist had put so much product in it that it felt crunchy. But he couldn't fault the shave, he mused, rubbing his palms on his baby-smooth cheeks. And his feet and hands looked great.

"Hi, Thom."

He glanced up to see ten-year-old Charlie Ross standing in front of him, dressed in a Minnesota Blizzard T-shirt and ragged jeans. He carried a battered hockey stick and wore rollerblades instead of shoes.

"Hey, Charlie. How's it going?" Charlie was one of five or six boys in the neighborhood who lived and breathed hockey. In the winter, they played at a local park rink, but in the summer they swapped a puck for a tennis ball and played on a nearby dead-end street.

"We're going to play some street hockey. Do you want to play?"

"I can't. Not today."

"You got a haircut," Charlie said, sitting down beside him.

Thom smiled. "Yeah, I did. What do you think? Does it look good?"

Charlie studied him carefully, then nodded. "Yeah, it looks good. Not as nice as my flow." Charlie ran his hand over his shaggy hair. "I got it goin' on."

"You sure do," Thom said.

Charlie's expression shifted. "My mom heard on the news that they're looking to trade you. Is that true?"

Thom nodded. "I think it might be."

"You don't wanna go, do you?"

"No," Thom said. "And I'm doing everything I can to stay. But it might not be up to me." He noticed Malin watching them from the window and nodded at her.

"I hope you stay," Charlie said.

Charlie was growing up without a father, like Thom had. Thom had never set himself up as a role model, but he knew that Charlie looked up to him, and he hated to disappoint the kid. "Do you and the boys want to do the hockey camp again this summer?"

"Can we?"

"Yeah, I'll grab some applications when I'm at the practice rink. Let the other boys know. I'm not sure I'll be around to drive you back and forth like I was last summer, but I'll still spring for the registration fees."

"We can take the bus," Charlie said. He paused. "But I sure hope you can stay, Thom."

Thom nodded. "You better get out of here. Your friends are going to be waiting."

"You won't leave without saying goodbye, will you?" Charlie asked.

"No, I promise."

Charlie waved as he skated off. Thom watched until he disappeared around the corner, thinking back to when he'd met the kid. His father had just taken off, and Thom had introduced him to hockey to try to fill the void, just as someone had for him. Thom had always thought he'd be around to watch Charlie play high school hockey.

But after all that had happened, all the mistakes he'd made, Charlie could be just the latest person he'd failed.

THE SILENCE IN THE firehouse was occasionally broken by the soft whir of air conditioning or the sound of a horn from the street. Thom had come inside a few hours before, then gone upstairs to work out. She'd decided to let him deal with his issues alone and had gone to the office. She returned around five, but he'd still been holed up in the gym. Now it was nearly nine and they hadn't had dinner yet.

In truth, she should have realized that she'd pushed him too hard. But he'd seemed happy to oblige her for most of the day. Then, like a switch had been flipped, his mood had changed at the photo studio. He hadn't been happy about the fashion shoot, but her plan was already working.

Thom had collected over ninety thousand Twitter followers in less than two days. She'd decided to put up an Instagram account, as well, adding the few photos they'd already posted and a picture of Thom's new haircut. All the responses to his new style had been favorable, particularly among the female fans.

Now for phase two: show people the good man she'd

gotten a glimpse of the last couple of days. The one who gave money to struggling entrepreneurs, expecting only doughnuts in return. The one who sat on the stoop with a neighborhood kid and treated him like a friend.

Reaching into her bag, she pulled out the invitation to the St. Paul Children's Hospital benefit, which was two weeks away. Her contact at the hospital had let it slip that Thom had already donated a large sum to the charity, and that he was a regular volunteer. He deserved to go to the benefit, but her father had demanded that Thom lay low until the trade could be arranged. Showing up at the benefit would directly defy that order, but it would also show Thom as human.

Malin sighed. She wasn't even sure if she could get Thom to change his *socks* now, much less dress up in a tux and walk a red carpet into the benefit. Besides that, she'd have to find him a date.

Her to-do list was getting longer, and Malin wasn't sure that she had a cooperative subject any longer. Perhaps it was best to find out if she was wasting her time with all this. Pushing off the sofa, she gathered up her things and headed upstairs.

"Thom?" she called. The workout room was empty, but she noticed a door open next to the bathroom. Peering around the doorjamb, she found a stairway that led up to the roof. "Thom?"

Malin switched on a light and climbed the stairs, then pushed open the steel door at the top. She sighed softly as she stepped onto the rooftop deck, a warm breeze teasing her hair. She'd stepped into a perfect oasis in the middle of the city.

There were lush plants and flowers everywhere, along with a few potted trees that rustled in the wind. A privacy fence outlined the perimeter, which was lined with strings of lights twinkling against the night sky.

Malin walked past a pair of upholstered chaises, both of them large enough for two or three people. In fact, the rooftop looked like it was made for a romantic interlude, with comfortable sofas and even an iron bed draped with netting. All that was missing was the hot tub.

But as she moved closer to the front of the firehouse, she noticed a wavering blue glow coming from behind a row of plants and realized she shouldn't have sold him so short. She found Thom relaxing in the tub, his eyes closed, earbuds in his ears. His arms were stretched out along the edges of the tub, and his skin shone from the underwater lights.

Malin's gaze dropped lower, to the parts of his naked body that were hidden beneath the bubbling surface. Kicking off her flip-flops, she moved to the edge of the tub, then swung her legs over the edge and into the hot water.

Thom must have felt the movement of the water, because he opened his eyes and stared at her for a long moment. A shiver raced through her body, and she couldn't seem to drag her gaze from his.

"I know you're angry at me," she began. "And I'm sorry for trying to do too much at once."

"I'm sorry, too," he said.

"You are?"

Thom shook his head. "I've been trying to figure it out, and the closest I can get is that I'm angry at myself."

"Go on," she said.

He drew a deep breath before he continued. "I'll admit, I have a few rough edges, and I don't always behave the way I should in social situations. And I have this undeniable need to defy authority when it comes to my personal life. This has always confused me, because on the ice, I'm focused and professional, and I do what is asked of me."

"You do," she said.

For a while he was caught up in his thoughts, and he didn't speak. Malin waited, hoping that he wouldn't shut down before revealing more. To her relief, he continued, this time with an angry edge to his voice.

"I know who I am. At least, I thought I did. And I was good with that guy, and I understood him. But since you've come along, it's like the Thom Quinn I knew got lost. Now I'm not sure who I am or how I feel about myself."

"I'm not trying to change the man you are," Malin said. "I like that man."

"Then why the hair and the clothes and all the stuff we did today?" Thom asked.

"That's just what the public sees. It's—it's a costume you put on. Like when you put on your uniform and skates and step onto the ice. You become Tommy the Beast."

"I'm not sure who I am without The Beast," he said. "There might not be anything beneath that."

Malin heard the fear in his words. As tough as Thom appeared on the outside, there was a very vulnerable man beneath the image. "Oh, there's someone wonderful there," she said in a quiet voice. "I've met him. And I really do like him."

He searched her face as if to gauge the truth in her words. He didn't trust easily, but Malin could feel that last wall between them crumbling. And in that moment, it was all that mattered to her. To have his trust, and to give him hers in return.

"So, what do I need to say to get you out of those clothes and into the water?" Thom murmured.

"I'm sure you have your lines."

"Not one that a woman like you would respond to," he said. "Why do I always feel like an inept teenager when I'm close to you?"

Malin slipped into the water, the loose cotton skirt she wore billowing out around her. Grabbing the hem of her shirt, she pulled it up and over her head and tossed it onto the deck. The skirt came next, and she pulled it off, leaving her dressed in just her hot pink bra and panties.

They'd already spent an entire day together naked. There was no need to play coy. So a few seconds later, she wadded up her underwear and tossed the ball next to her skirt. Malin waited for a sign that he was ready for her.

It came in a rush as he rose out of the water and pulled her body against his. Malin had time for only a quick breath before his mouth came down on hers in a deep and desperate kiss.

He was like a man starved for the taste of her, his tongue delving deep. Malin felt her limbs go weak, and she reached up to wrap her arms around his neck.

Thom pulled her down into the water, breaking the bubbling surface. Every touch, every sensation seemed heightened by the water on her skin, as if it was conducting electricity that pulsed to her fingertips and toes.

"I can't get enough of you," he murmured as they came up for air, his lips finding the tip of each breast and teasing the nipples.

Malin tipped her head back and lost herself in the wild sensations coursing through her. She was about to make love to Thom Quinn, and there wasn't a single doubt in her mind that it was the right thing to do.

Thom pulled her legs around his waist and their bodies came together, his stiff shaft caught between them, pressing against her belly. Malin moved against him, and the tip of his penis slipped between her legs.

She needed to feel him deep inside her, filling her with the heat of his body. But at the same time, Malin wanted to wait, to savor every moment they had together. Determined to make him ache for release, she drew him to his feet so he was out of the water and then slowly slid down, pressing her lips along a delicious trail from his collarbone to the soft hair beneath his belly button.

Malin ran her tongue along the length of his shaft. His reaction was sharp and intense, a gasp slipping from his lips as he groaned. And when she took him into her mouth, Thom furrowed his damp fingers through her hair.

As she stroked him with her tongue, Malin watched his desire grow. Several times he stopped her, holding tight to hair as he fought with self-control. And when he couldn't take any more, Thom drew her up to her feet, slipped his hands beneath her, and wrapped her legs around his waist.

He swung his legs over the side of the tub and carried her over to a chaise, gently dropping her onto the soft surface. Then he fetched his shorts and a blanket from a nearby chair.

Malin watched as he pulled a condom out of his wallet and handed it to her.

"How long has that been in there?" she asked.

"Since this morning," he admitted with a shy grin.

"So you were pretty sure you were going to get lucky today?"

"Am I about to get lucky?" Thom asked.

"Depends on what you consider lucky."

"You, naked, smiling at me and holding a condom. I'd say I'm pretty damn close."

5

WOULD IT ALWAYS feel like the first time?

A few days later, they were stretched out on a rooftop chaise that he'd pulled beneath the awning, protecting them both from the hot midday sun. The breeze cooled their sticky skin and set the filmy curtains to dancing around them.

Malin shifted, her bare legs sliding up to circle his hips. He knew what came next, the exquisite sensation of disappearing into her body, the warmth that surrounded him, the first incredible sensations as he began to move inside her. And then each stroke, bringing them both closer to release.

Thom had always believed he understood sex. He knew exactly how to bring a woman to the edge with his tongue or his fingers or his cock. But with Malin, he'd come to realize that that end goal was just scratching the surface. There were so many other experiences that had nothing to do with release.

She smoothed the condom over his shaft, her fingers firm against his heat. Thom understood the need for protection, but that didn't keep him from wondering what it would feel like with nothing between them.

He rolled over and slid into her with one stroke. She arched against him, a silent invitation to drive deeper. Thom bent closer and ran his tongue along the crease of her mouth. Malin opened her eyes and smiled at him. "I don't know if I can do this again," she murmured.

He'd taken her over the top twice already, but Thom Quinn was not about to leave his woman unsatisfied. He reached between them and found the spot that made her gasp, then gently flicked his finger over the soft fold of flesh.

Malin moaned softly, and he began to move again. He watched her expression shift, first to pleasure, then to sweet torment. He knew what do to make her come, knew exactly how to carry her to the heights and then let her drop into pleasure.

After a week together, he'd studied everything about her, all the details that made Malin so incredibly captivating. Silly things like how she'd burrow through a pint of ice cream like a miner, digging out all the toffee or cherries before eating any of the ice cream. Or how she'd spend ten minutes brushing her teeth, insisting that it was the only way to make sure they were perfectly clean.

And when she slept, he knew when she was caught in a dream because of the nonsensical words and the tossing and turning. Then he'd gather her in his arms and draw her against his body and she'd grow instantly calm.

Every day it was something new, something more

fascinating, and Thom had to wonder how long this feeling would last. The thought of losing her before he discovered everything about her caused an ache deep inside him.

He closed his eyes and focused on the spot where their bodies were joined. Slowly, rational thought dissolved in his mind and pure sensation took over. Thom drove deep, then drew back slowly until the connection between them was nearly broken. Again and he felt her fingertips dig into his hips. Again and she gasped his name.

Suddenly her body jerked, and Thom felt the spasms overwhelm her body. He lasted just a few seconds more until his own pleasure became undeniable. This time, the descent lasted longer, each of them completely drained of energy when it ended.

He collapsed beside her, pulling her body against his until she was as close as she could be. He pressed his lips against her shoulder and she sighed.

"At some point, we're going to have to leave this apartment," Malin murmured.

"Why? We send out for most of our meals. You can work from home. And think of all the money we can save on clothes."

"And what about your hockey career?" Malin asked.

"I figure by the time next season starts, I'll either be dead from exhaustion or ready to assume my new position as Supreme Sex God."

Malin giggled. "And I suppose as Supreme Sex God you'll be expected to service other women?"

"I suppose I will," he said.

She rolled over and stretched out on top of him, pinning his arms over his head. "Then I suppose I'm going to have to do everything I can to exhaust you."

"Promise?"

Malin then folded her arms across his chest and rested her chin on her hands. "I'm serious, though. We can't spend the entire summer in this apartment."

"We won't if I get traded."

Her gaze met his, and he saw the certainty in her eyes. "I hope that doesn't happen," she said.

"I know," Thom said. "And I appreciate everything you're doing to help me. But I'm not sure I'm ready for another spa day."

"So, what can we do for fun? There has to be something."

"Well, I have a cabin up near Mille Lacs Lake. We could go up there for a week."

"Is there Wi-Fi?" Malin asked.

"There's no running water, no indoor plumbing and no electricity," he said.

"I have to be able to do my work. And as much as I'd love to be stranded in the wilderness with you, I require indoor plumbing."

"All right. We could leave the country. No one would recognize me in Mexico or the Caribbean. We could go to Belize. I'm sure they'd have Wi-Fi at the resorts."

"Then there's always Europe," Malin suggested. "Paris and Rome."

"Ireland," Thom said.

"Norway," Malin added. She drew a deep breath.

"But we're not going to be one hundred percent safe anywhere. All it takes is one person with a cell phone."

"Would it be so bad if we got caught?" Thom asked.

"Maybe not for me, but believe me, my father would find a way to destroy you."

"So? I can't play hockey forever."

"Why would you want to quit? You have a lot of good years of hockey left."

"Sure, but I could just as easily be injured and have to quit. No matter what, hockey wasn't going to be my life."

Malin ran her fingertips across his chest. "I know how hard it is for some guys. They've played hockey for their entire lives. They aren't prepared or qualified to do anything else. And when it's all over, their whole world changes. What will you do?"

"Honestly? I'm not sure," he said.

"Well, I suppose if the whole Supreme Sex God thing works out for you, that's fine. But aren't you going to want to get up and have some kind of purpose to your day?"

"I'll get it all figured out someday," Thom said. That sounded way more optimistic than he felt. But he wanted to keep his options open. If there was even an infinitesimal chance that Malin would still be in his life, then that changed everything.

"Until then, I have a plan for today. I know a guy who has a private ice arena. Sometimes I use it to train in the summer when I don't want to go to the team rink. Why don't we pick up your skates and we'll go get a little exercise on the ice?"

Malin rolled off him, sitting on her knees, her body still flushed from their early morning activities. "I don't have skates," she said. "I don't really need them since I never learned to skate."

"Your dad owned a hockey team and he never got you out on the ice?"

"I was a girl. Girls don't play hockey. At least, that's what my dad thinks."

"Girls do play hockey," Thom said. "And I guess I'm going to have to be the one to teach you."

"All right. But we've got to buy some skates. And I'll need a stick. And I definitely need a helmet. And lots of padding in case I fall down."

"We'll take care of that," Thom said. "But first, a shower, then breakfast, then skating."

"I'm excited," Malin said. "My brothers played hockey and I always wanted to learn. Instead, I got ballet and riding lessons."

He crawled out of bed and pulled her to her feet beside him. "You can ride a horse?"

"I can ride a horse while it's jumping over a fence," Malin said.

Thom wrapped his arm around her waist and brought her close to his body. "Well, that explains everything."

Malin frowned. "What does it explain?"

He led her to the bathroom, then turned on the shower to warm it up. He sat her down on the edge of the tub and looked at the cut on her head. "Almost healed."

"What does it explain?" Malin asked again.

"Why you're so good at sex," he said.

She gasped, then reached out to give him a playful punch to his shoulder. But Thom grabbed her and picked her up off her feet, carrying her into the huge marble shower. She screamed and giggled as he held her under the shower head, drenching her hair and body in just moments.

Slowly he loosened his grip and she slid down, the water providing lubrication between their naked bodies. When her feet finally reached the floor, she smiled, then pressed a kiss to the center of his chest. But to his surprise, she continued down, trailing her lips from his chest to his groin.

Thom groaned softly, awaiting the feel of her soft lips and warm tongue. Ice skating could wait. Maybe until they were old and feeble and uninterested in sex. It could be years, he thought as he leaned back against the wall of the shower. Years and years.

MALIN SAT AT the breakfast bar, sipping at a mug of coffee as she paged through the Sunday sports section. It was summer, so most of the news focused on major league baseball, but there was a small article about trade possibilities for the Blizzard.

Of course, Thom's name was front and center, but there was a small reference to some indecision on management's part. She and Thom had slowly been posting more of the photos, as well as some candid ones she'd taken around the house. His followers seemed to eat them up, and she hoped the team's management was taking notice. She scanned the article again, wondering who on the management team was having second thoughts. It would be nice to have an ally in her plan to save Thom's career, someone to trust.

"Hey. How long have you been up?"

"About an hour," she said.

Thom walked into the room, dressed in faded cargo shorts that hung low on his narrow hips. His hair, still wet from the shower, stuck up in unruly spikes. Though she'd taught him how to style it, he rarely took the time do much beyond rubbing it dry with a towel.

Thom wrapped his arms around her from behind, nuzzling her neck, his breath warm on her skin. "Good morning."

Malin sighed softly as his lips found a spot below her ear. "Good morning."

He sat down next to her, then reached for her mug and took a long sip. "You're all dressed up."

"I went out to Nirvana and got doughnuts," she said, pointing at the turquoise box. "Nora says hello, and she also wanted to thank you for the Twitter mention. Business has been crazy."

Thom opened the box and pulled out one of his favorites—a lemon-glazed poppy seed doughnut. Malin slid off the stool and fetched the coffeepot and a fresh mug for him. "I need to go into the office today. I called Drew, and he's going to meet me there and take out my stitches."

"I can take them out," Thom said, his mouth full of doughnut. "I take out my own stitches all the time."

"Thanks, but I'll stick with the real doctor," Malin said.

Thom held out a piece of his doughnut, and she took a bite. "What else do you have to do?" he asked.

"My dad is usually around for a few hours on Sunday mornings. I wanted to see if I could get anything out of him about their progress on a trade." She pointed to the article in the paper. "Here, read this."

Malin watched as he scanned the column. Finally he looked up and shrugged. "It's nothing new."

"But it is. It sounds like someone is breaking ranks and rejecting the idea of a trade. Here, read this over again."

Thom did as he was told but still shook his head. "How do you know they aren't talking about you?"

Malin scoffed at the notion. "No one in that office or in the press considers me part of the management team. I just have to find out who is crossing over to our side and work with him."

He munched on his doughnut as she went through her phone messages, but when she looked up, he was still staring at her.

"What?" Malin asked.

"You're going to leave me all alone here? I thought one of your primary job duties was to keep a sharp eye on me."

Malin set her phone down on the counter and studied him shrewdly. "Are you planning to go out and get drunk and cause trouble today?"

"No," Thom said.

"Are you planning to pick up a bunch of women and take pictures of yourself half-naked?"

"No," he said. Thom reached for his phone and held

it up, snapping a photo of her. "Well, maybe not a group of women, but there is this one chick who makes me kind of crazy. You want to see her photo?"

"Chick? I've been reduced to juvenile poultry?" Malin asked.

"All right, what am I supposed to call you?" Thom asked. "We've spent a week together, most of it in bed. We're kind of doing the relationship thing. I think you like me and I certainly like you. A few labels might be helpful."

"You like me?"

Thom cursed beneath his breath. "If I haven't made that perfectly clear, then I'm doing something wrong. I could take you back to bed and prove it to you."

"The only thing that would prove is that you enjoy having sex," Malin teased.

He stood up, then turned her around on the stool so she faced him. Dropping a quick kiss on her lips, he pressed his forehead to hers. "It's different with you," he murmured. "It's not just sex."

Malin closed her eyes. They hadn't really talked about their relationship beyond their sexual desires for each other. As long as they were still in the discovery phase, she figured they didn't have to.

In truth, Malin was afraid to talk about the future. If she didn't manage to save his job, then he'd be gone by the end of the summer. And if she did, there was no way she could explain a relationship with the team's bad boy—the one she'd been assigned to watch—to her father.

For now, it was best to take things one day at a time.

They were single adults able to enjoy each other both in and out of bed. Wasn't that enough? She didn't want any promises. "Maybe you should start to think of me as one of your puck bunnies," she murmured.

He sucked in a sharp breath, then stepped back from her. "What the hell are you saying? I've never treated you like one of those girls."

She could read the anger in his eyes and wished she could take back her words. "You haven't. I was just suggesting that we should keep things simple between us."

Malin could almost see him withdraw from her, his walls going up faster than she would have ever imagined. She felt a surge of pain so strong it took her breath away. Obviously Thom had been more invested in what was happening between them than she'd realized. "I'm sorry," she said. "Forget I said that. It came out all wrong."

"No, you're right," Thom interrupted. "Simple is best. Hell, I don't know where I'll be next month or the month after that. And you have a lot more important things to do in your life than hanging around with a guy like me."

"A guy like you?" Malin frowned. "What is that supposed to mean?"

"A messed up hockey player. Come on, Malin, you can admit it. If someone had told you last month that you'd be sleeping with a dumb hockey player, you would have told them they were crazy."

"You're probably right," she said. "But as strange as

it sounds, I really don't think of you as a hockey player. I just think of you as…Thom Quinn."

"Not Tommy the Beast?"

"No," Malin said, shaking her head. "That's just some silly character you play on the ice. That much was clear from the start." Malin reached up and cupped his face between her hands, placing a soft but lingering kiss on his lips. "Are we all right?"

"Yeah," Thom said, nodding. "We're cool." But the words were clipped.

Malin hopped off the stool. "I have to get over to the office. I should be back in a few hours."

"I've got some things I have to do today, too," Thom said. "I'm meeting up with my brothers later. We're have dinner at Nana's. I'll be gone when you get back."

"All right. So, I'll see you…when I see you," she said with an awkward smile.

Malin grabbed her things, gave him another kiss, then hurried out of the firehouse. Her car was parked in front at the curb, and she got inside and turned the key in the ignition. But as she drove toward the office, she found her thoughts occupied with the conversation she'd just had.

This had all started with her decision to help Thom shed his beastly persona. He would save his career and she would make hers. That had been the plan. But she had to admit that Thom had been right when he'd said part of that plan was to impress her father. A part of her had thought she could make Thom over into the kind of man her father might admire. Now she realized how naive that had been. Davis Pedersen loved his players, but he never thought of them as anything more than just commodities that could be sacrificed and traded one for another in the name of profit. And perhaps he would never think of her any differently, either.

When she got downtown, the streets were quiet. She pulled into the parking garage of the team's headquarters. She noticed her father's car parked in its reserved spot next to the elevator. As she walked inside, Malin thought about what she was going to say to him.

During the hockey season, the office was usually buzzing with activity from dawn until just before midnight. The team had made a commitment to be the fan-friendliest franchise in the league, and that meant careful attention to the team website as well as all the other traditional media in town.

Malin's job focused on new media. But she often helped with larger projects like the team's annual fan convention, BlizzardCon, held the last week of August. As she walked to her office, she noticed that Natalie, one of the assistants in the special events department, was hard at work at her desk.

"Hi, Nat," Malin said.

"Malin! Hey there. Where have you been? Vacation?"

"No, I've just been working from home. I hit my head pretty hard, and I wanted to be careful in case I had a concussion," Malin said. That much was true. "What have you got going?"

"BlizzardCon, what else? Oh, and Ray gave me the hospital benefit. I'm trying to find some players to attend, but most of them have left town. I've got two confirmed so far—Jake Weston and Devin McAllen. Not exactly the kind of guys who can make polite chit-chat with high profile guests. I can dress them up in a tuxedo and bow tie, but if they show up without their teeth, the photos are going to be horrendous."

"What about Thom Quinn?" Malin said. "He's a core player, good-looking, and can carry on a conversation."

"He's a total hottie," Natalie said. "But we got a memo that said we're not to assign him any appearances. It looks like he's up to be traded. Too bad, since he's here in town and actually from the Twin Cities."

"And he's done more volunteer work for the hospital than any other player," Malin murmured.

"He has?"

"Yeah. I heard he's over there all the time. He just prefers to go when the cameras are gone. He donated the money to redo their third-floor playroom, and he helped build it."

Natalie smiled. "I didn't know that," she said. "I suppose I could give him a call. Or you could do a girl a favor and call him for me? An invite coming from the owner's daughter might be more persuasive than one from some lowly assistant."

"All right," Malin said. "I'll see if I can convince him."

"Are you going?"

"I was planning to. What about you?"

"I have a killer dress, but I don't have a date. And those things can be so weird when you go alone."

"I'll be there without a date," Malin said. "You can

sit with me. Call and make sure we're at the same table. It'll be fun."

"All right, I will. Thanks."

Malin gave her a little wave, then continued down the hall to her father's office. She knocked on the door as she walked inside.

Davis Pedersen sat at his desk, dressed in a bright blue golf shirt and plaid trousers.

"Hi, Daddy."

"Malin. I'm surprised to see you here on a Sunday."

"I've been working from home this last week. I thought I'd stop by and go through my mail."

He glanced up at her, then stared at her for a long moment. Malin forced a smile, wondering what it was he found displeasing about her appearance. She smoothed her hands over the loose peasant skirt she wore, then quickly checked to see if she'd spilled coffee on her T-shirt.

"What is it?" she asked.

"Nothing," he said. "You—you just look…"

"How do I look?"

He narrowed his eyes, then shook his head. "Different."

Malin swallowed hard. There was no way he could tell that she'd been spending her days and nights being well-pleasured by Thom Quinn. Could he? Well, if he asked, she'd give him the truth.

She crossed the room and sat down in one of the leather chairs in front of his desk. "What's going on with the Quinn trade? Has there been any interest from other teams?"

"Why are you asking?"

"Did you forget? I'm supposed to make sure he doesn't get in any trouble. You're the one who assigned me that job. And he's been a model player for the last week. He's even joined Twitter, and he's amassing quite the loyal following."

"Yes, yes," he said. "I got your first report."

"Good. Now, what about the trade?"

Davis Pedersen leaned forward, resting his arms on his desk. "It's going to happen. New York is interested, and they have a few players we could use. And we're still talking to Vancouver."

"You're never going to get back what he's really worth to this team," Malin said.

"What do you know about his value?"

"I know that he overcame a pretty horrible childhood to make a success of himself. The odds were against him making anything of his life, and he managed to learn the game of hockey and become one of the best in the league. I also know he's a hometown guy with a lot of fans out there who would be heartbroken at a trade."

"You seem to be very familiar with the guy," her father said.

"I've made a point to find out more about him. And this whole Tommy the Beast image doesn't represent who he really is. Maybe you should meet with him, Daddy. Talk to him, get to know him. I think you might realize that trading him would be a mistake."

"Enough," he said. "You've made your feelings very

clear and I appreciate your insight, but I'm not going to waste any more time discussing it."

"Fine," Malin said. "I guess I'll see you at the hospital benefit this weekend."

"You're going?"

"I am. And I'm bringing a date. He's a doctor. You'll love him. We will have a spot at your table, won't we?"

"I'm sure your mother can arrange it," he said.

"Good. I'll call her just to be sure." Malin stood up and circled the desk, then gave her father a kiss on the cheek. "Bye, Daddy. Love you."

His expression softened slightly, and he gave her a grudging smile. "Love you, too, Linny."

As she walked out of the office, Malin smiled to herself. If her father refused to meet with Thom, then she'd find a way for Thom to meet him. What better place than the hospital benefit? She'd reserve a place for her "date" and when he had to cancel, she'd invite Thom to sit in his place. Oh, and she'd have to remember to tell Natalie not to arrange for Thom to be sitting with her.

It was a good plan, except for the fact that she still had to convince Thom to attend. If she knew anything about him, a stuffy benefit dinner with lots of cameras was the last place he'd want to be. But Malin knew if she'd managed to convince The Beast to get a mani-pedi, surely she could convince him to put on a bow tie…

THERE WEREN'T MANY traditions that had taken hold in Thom's family. Holidays often passed by without any fanfare. When he was younger, birthdays had been ignored because his parents had never had the money for presents or even a store-bought cake. But one tradition had stuck with Thom, his older brother, Tristan, and his younger brother, James: Sunday dinner with their grandmother.

The state had turned the brothers over to their grandmother as a last resort when they were in their late teens. And though she appeared to be fragile and sickly at the time, the responsibilities of caring for three difficult boys had given Irene Forsberg a new lease on life. She'd turned out to be the only family member they could depend upon, besides each other.

When they were younger, they'd gathered at Nana's house every Sunday. But now that the trio all had full-time careers, they visited Irene on the first Sunday of every month. They'd spend the morning working through her list of chores and the afternoon at the dinner table, getting stuffed with homemade food.

"What's this I hear about a trade?" Tristan asked as he and Thom were working on repairing Irene's front steps.

Thom pulled off the leather gloves he was wearing and sat down on the top step. "They haven't been too keen on my off-ice behavior. That post-playoff trip to Vegas went over like a turd sandwich. The pictures were posted everywhere."

"They're going to trade you because of a few pictures?"

"And something that never happened with a teenage hooker. Remind me never again to do a good deed for a stranger, even if she is a starving kid."

His younger brother, James, stepped out of the house, three beers carried between his fingers. He handed one to each of his older brothers, then stretched out in a wicker chair on the porch. "Did you ask him about the trade?"

Tris nodded. "He says it's true."

"It's true," Thom said, nodding.

"You all right with that?" James asked.

"I guess I don't have much choice," Thom said. "I want to stay near you guys and Nana, and I promise I'll never go so far that I can't come home."

"Thom, if you have to leave Minneapolis, none of us will feel like you're abandoning us. We know you're not Dad, or Mom, for that matter."

At his brother's words, a weight lifted from Thom's shoulders that he hadn't even realized was there. "Thanks, Tris. I got myself into this mess. And now I have to deal with the consequences."

"What's the worst that could happen?" Tris asked.

"They could trade me to a crappy team. They could banish me to the minors, although they'd have to eat a multimillion-dollar contract. I doubt they'd be keen on that." He shrugged. "I've been getting some help from the social media director for the team. She's polishing me up a bit, hoping to get rid of the bad boy image."

"You're Tommy the bloody Beast," Tris said. "If you're not him, who will you be?"

"I don't know. Someone who behaves like a responsible adult. A role model. Someone they might want to keep on the team."

Jamie took a swig of his beer. "We could always sue

them," he said. "The guys at my firm are going to be pissed off if you get traded. I could talk to someone in our legal department."

"Nope. I'm good," Thom said. "I've learned that if I want people to see the real me, I have to be real. And that means accepting whatever happens. And I'll live with it."

"Jesus," Jamie cried. "What has happened to our brother? He's gone soft inside. Are you concerned, Tristan?"

"I am, James," Tristan said in mock seriousness. "Maybe if we fill him full of liquor, he'll tell us what's really going on."

"That's going to take a boatload of beer, brother. Give me your wallet, Thom. I'll go buy some more beer."

Thom held up his hands. "I don't need your help, and I'm taking it easy on the liquor," he said. "But I could use a bit of advice."

"I can advise you about the law," Jamie said.

"And if you've got real estate questions, I'm you're guy."

"This is about a woman," Thom ventured.

"I'm out," Tris said.

"Me, too."

"You don't even know what I want to talk about."

"You're the one with all the women," Jamie said. "Man, I should have worked harder at hockey. No one wants to date a lawyer. You should ask Tris. He had a girlfriend a few months back. She stuck around for a while."

"I could only fool her for so long," Tris said with a chuckle. "Once she had me figured out, she was gone."

"This is the problem," Thom said. "We've all had messed up attempts at relationships. But…"

"But?" Jamie asked.

"But maybe it's all about meeting the right woman. I think all those problems go away when you find the right…fit."

Tristan and James stared at him, brows furrowed, doubt in their eyes. "Nah, it can't be that simple," James said.

"It might be," Thom said. "This girl—this woman—is complicated and smart and beautiful, and she thinks I'm the same. I keep worrying she's going to see the real me and walk away. But when she does, it doesn't seem to make a difference to her. God, I don't want to mess this up. But I can't help feeling it's going to go to hell sooner or later."

"Why?" Tristan asked. "Maybe your theory is right."

"If I get traded, she won't be coming with me. And if I stay here, I'm not sure I can even date her. She's the daughter of the club's owner."

"You're dating the boss's daughter?" Tristan asked.

Thom winced. "Yeah. Only we're not really dating. Right now, we spend most of our time in bed. And we can't be seen in public. But so far, other than that, it's going very well."

"Is this one of those instances when you complain about something and we're supposed to feel sorry for you, when in reality you're bragging and we're supposed to feel jealous?" Tris asked.

Thom took a long sip of his beer. "No. I was just hoping for some insight."

Jamie cleared his throat. "Here's some insight, big brother. If you're really falling for this girl, you're going to have to think seriously about where this is leading. Relationships are not just about having a woman there to tell you how wonderful you are or to keep your bed warm. You're talking about marriage. And kids. And fifty years together. Are you really ready for that?"

Silence fell over the trio on the porch before Tris cursed softly. "Leave it to James to find the dark side in every happy moment."

"Hey, I'm just being honest. We're all in the same boat. After what we went through as kids, none of us is equipped to make marriage work. The sooner we admit that, the better."

"I don't believe it," Thom said. "I'm not going to just give up on finding happiness. If you're going to do that, then what is your life really worth?" He pushed to his feet. "I've got to go. I'll see you guys later."

Thom pulled open the screen door and walked inside his grandmother's house. He found her in the kitchen, taking a tray of cookies out of the oven. "Are you finished in the yard?" she asked.

"Almost. Tris and Jamie are going to finish up. I have to get going."

"Let me pack up some of these cookies," she said. "They're peanut butter. Your favorite."

"Thanks, Nana," Thom said. He stepped around

the kitchen island and pulled his grandmother into a gentle hug. The Quinn boys had never been very demonstrative, so he wasn't surprised to see the shock on his grandmother's face.

"If I haven't told you lately, you saved us all. We should have come to you sooner."

"If only I had known you boys were in trouble, I would have brought you here in a heartbeat." Her eyes filled with tears. "I blame your mother for pushing me so far away I didn't come looking for you until it was almost too late."

"No blame," Thom said. "We're all healthy and happy. We made it through."

She reached up and pressed her palm to his cheek. "You are a dear boy. And I hope you know how heartbroken I'd be if they sent you to another team. I like having you close."

Thom hugged her again. "I'll be heartbroken, too, but it's time I took responsibility for what I've done. And I'll be back in the off-season," he said.

She tipped her head up as she scrutinized him. "I'm happy to hear that but…is everything else all right?"

"Sure."

"There's something different about you. I'm not sure what it is." She brushed his hair back, then paused. "Contentment," she finally said. "You look content."

"Maybe I am," Thom said. "Maybe I am."

He grabbed the box of cookies and brushed a kiss onto his grandmother's cheek, then left her to the rest of her baking.

When he reached the porch, Jamie and Tris were in

the middle of an argument over Jamie's new car, and like most of the arguments between the brothers, it would probably end in a wrestling match.

"Later," Thom called as he headed for his truck.

But neither of them seemed to notice him leaving. He hopped in his truck and wove through the old St. Paul neighborhood. He'd bought the house for his grandmother after he signed his first free-agent contract with the club. He and his brothers had spent nearly five months rehabbing the place.

They'd moved her in on Christmas Eve, bringing her home to a fully furnished home, complete with a Christmas tree. He smiled at the memory. Not every moment from his past had been bleak and filled with sadness. He just had to seek out the happiness and stay focused on that.

When he got to his car, he dialed Malin's number and waited for her to pick up. "Hey there," he said when he heard her voice. "I'm on my way home and I wondered if you wanted me to pick up dinner."

"I've got everything covered," Malin said. "I did a big grocery shop on my way home."

He knew she'd spent the day at the office, but Thom was afraid to ask her whom she'd seen. "How was your day?" he ventured.

"Interesting," Malin said. "I'll tell you later. By the way, you now have over two hundred thousand Twitter followers. Pretty big numbers for just one week."

"Great," he murmured. He wasn't quite sure what those numbers meant, but if they made Malin happy, then he was all for it. "I'll be home in a few minutes."

He tossed the phone on the passenger seat and pulled away from the curb. Home. It had always just been the place where he kept his stuff, a place to sleep and a place to get his mail. But since Malin had moved in, the firehouse had become something more. He looked forward to walking in the front door and finding her there.

Oh, hell, he was in so deep, Thom had to wonder if he'd ever find his way out.

6

On Wednesday, Thom flopped down on the sofa beside Malin, holding a bowl of soup that he'd purchased from a local deli. "Are you sure you don't want some of this?" he asked.

"Not now," she murmured, staring down at her iPad. "I have to get this work done. I'm way behind."

"You have the perfect job," he said. "You could be lying on some beach and still be able to do your job."

"I suppose I could," Malin said. "But I wouldn't have you there to keep interrupting me."

Thom frowned. He knew she was teasing. After nearly two weeks with her, he'd learned a lot about Malin Pedersen. He could read her moods as easily as he could read a newspaper. And right now, she was slightly irritated about the amount of work she had left to do. She was also worried about something she didn't want to talk about. Thom suspected it had to do with the trade hanging over his head. Though she'd worked hard to marshal the power of social media,

Thom wasn't sure it was making a difference. The number of followers he was gaining had slowed, even. Malin had insisted that he post twice a day and had recently given him a poll to send out on whether he should stay or go.

Of course, the results weren't difficult to guess. Only seven percent wanted him to go, and Malin explained that those votes probably came from fans of Blizzard competitors.

"I'll be done in fifteen minutes," she said. "Why don't you do some laundry? Or work out?"

"I could go buy you some skates," he said. "I really want to get back on the ice. It's been almost three weeks."

She set her tablet down and focused her attention on him for a moment. "I completely trust you to go out on your own."

"I don't want to go alone. I want you to come with me," he said. "Who will take the photo for social media if you're not there?"

"Go!" she shouted.

"No, I think I'll just finish my lunch and hang around here."

She gave him a dirty look and he took the hint. He'd just have to figure out another way to find out what was bothering her.

MALIN SHOOK HER head as Thom headed for the kitchen. She'd wondered if the day would come when she wanted some time to herself, and she realized that the "honeymoon" they'd been on was coming to an end.

She'd let her work slide to the point that she was now three or four days behind.

Or maybe she was just reacting to a severe lack of sleep. After another passionate night together, she'd been left with only four hours of sleep.

Her phone rang. She picked it up, and a Snapchat of a naked and very muscular chest appeared.

There was no question as to who the chest belonged to. "Thom!"

He didn't answer, and the picture disappeared from her screen, only to be replaced a few moments later by a close up of his abs, finely carved into a perfect six-pack. "Do not send me a dick pic," she shouted.

Her phone beeped again and she didn't even want to look. With a soft curse, Malin tossed the papers off her lap and began to search the house for him. She found him in the workout room, taking a picture of his butt in the mirror on the wall.

"Who taught you how to use Snapchat?" she asked, her hands on her waist, her expression as fierce as she could manage.

"I taught myself," he said. "The question is, why didn't you tell me about it? It's really quite useful. Do you know the pictures disappear after five seconds?"

"That's what they tell you," Malin said. "But there are so many ways around that. I want you to take that app off your phone."

"I will only use it to send stuff to you," he promised.

"That would be fine in theory. But then, one day, you're going to get distracted and press the wrong button and you'll post an obscene photo on your Twitter feed and the whole world will get a peek at your bits and pieces."

He froze, his gaze fixed on hers. "Could that happen?"

"You'd better give me that phone right now," Malin said, holding out her hand.

He did as he was told, and she checked to make sure he hadn't made any blunders. To her relief, he hadn't. She dumped the app, deleted the pictures then handed his phone back to him. "And you haven't posted anything to Twitter today?"

"I was going to take a photo of my soup, but then I ate it," he said.

"Say something about your workout," she said. "We should at least pretend you're keeping in shape."

Her phone rang again and she sighed, shaking her head. "What now?" Malin read the text message and smiled. "Delivery. I think it's my dress!"

"Dress?"

Malin raced down the stairs and then through the main floor to the front door. A delivery man stood out front, holding a huge box. He handed her a clipboard and she signed the receipt, then took the box from his outstretched arms. "Thank you."

Malin turned to find Thom standing behind her. "Who sent you a dress?"

"A friend of mine in New York. A designer. I needed something to wear for the hospital benefit this weekend."

"The benefit for the children's hospital?" Thom asked.

"Yes. The team does a lot of charity work for them. Of course, you know that. You've been there before, haven't you?"

Thom nodded. "Sure. Lots of times."

Malin had decided to take a different approach to get Thom to go to the gala. Instead of demanding that he attend the event and forcing him into a tuxedo, she was hoping a little reverse psychology would do the trick.

"You're going alone?" he asked.

"No," she said. "I'll have to find myself a date, I'm sure. But that shouldn't be too hard. I was going to ask Drew. He'd probably like to go."

"The team doctor?"

"Yeah." Malin set the box down on the table and opened it, then brushed back the layers of tissue paper. Looping her fingers through the shoulder straps, she slowly lifted the dress out of the box and held it in front of her.

It was the most spectacular gown she'd ever seen. Heavily beaded and fitted to the body, the garnet color was perfect against her pale skin. Without even trying it on, she could tell the neckline was daring, but she wanted a dress that would make a statement.

"You can't ask Drew," Thom said.

"Why not?"

"Because he already has the hots for you. Once he sees you in that dress, it will be all over."

"But I need a date."

"I got an invite," Thom said. "We could go together."

Malin forced back a smile and pretended to consider

his offer. "Oh, you don't have to do that. Besides, how did you get a personal invitation?"

"I've helped out a lot at the hospital outside of team events," he said. "They sent me an invitation directly."

"You didn't mention that. Were you going to go?"

"No. I normally don't care for events like that. I usually just send a big donation. But I guess I could go this time. It would be worth it just to see you in that dress."

"We wouldn't be able to go together," she said. "But we could meet there. Maybe I could get you a spot at our table."

"Let's just leave it at drinks and a few dances, shall we? I don't want to start some gossip. There are bound to be photographers there."

Malin could barely control her delight. How could this be so simple? She'd expected to have to do more to convince him to come. Another roadblock might be in order. "You'll need a tux. And not a rental. You'll have to buy one and get it fitted. Are you willing to do that?"

"I have a tux," he said. "A real nice one."

Malin watched as he disappeared into the bedroom. A minute later he returned with a garment bag. She unzipped the front and took out a beautiful jacket with matching trousers. The designer name on the inside was proof enough that Thom did indeed have a proper tuxedo. "Very nice. When did you get this?"

"I dated an actress for about three weeks during awards season. I went to one of the ceremonies during the all-star break, and she got the tux for me. They just hand out free clothes at those award ceremonies. I have a shirt, too, and studs and cuff links. Even shoes. The whole deal."

"Then I guess there's no reason for you not to go," Malin said.

He slipped his hands around her waist. "I think you should try that dress on and let me get a look at it."

"No," Malin said, playfully slipping out of his embrace. "You're going to have to wait."

"How are we going to handle this? Unless you're wearing a potato sack, I'm going to have a hard time keeping my hands off you."

"You're going to have to gather your resolve and do your best," Malin teased. "My parents will be there, and most of the management team. I'm sure they're going to be keeping a close eye on you."

Thom grew silent, and Malin knew exactly what he was thinking. His position with the Blizzard was still up in the air. On misstep could ruin everything. But that's why she wanted him to go. "This will be a great opportunity to show them that you're a lot more than just Tommy the Beast."

"There is one more thing I'm concerned about," he said.

"Besides my dress?"

Thom nodded. "I can't dance. I mean, I can move if I'm drunk enough, and everyone else is drunk enough. If the lights are low, it maybe resembles dancing. But the kind of dancing they do at these events is beyond my capabilities."

Malin took his hand, then twirled beneath it. "I guess I'm going to have to teach you."

"JUST RELAX," MALIN SAID. "Try to think of it as having sex, only fully clothed and standing upright. And move to the beat of the music."

Thom bit back a curse and tried to calm his frustration. This was his third attempt at a dancing lesson. The first had ended after five minutes, when he'd stepped on Malin's foot and she refused to continue. Their second attempt didn't go much better. He couldn't seem to get the hang of moving to the beat of the music, especially when Malin switched the count from one-two to one-two-three.

She wore a loose cotton dress, thin enough that he could feel every curve beneath. Thom knew she wasn't wearing anything beneath the dress. He'd seen her pull it on. And he knew how easy it would be to tug it over her head and expose her naked body to the moonlight.

"Be patient," she said. "You're trying too hard."

"There is no such thing as trying too hard. If you don't try, you'll never master anything. And if you don't try hard, it will take forever."

They'd eaten a late supper up on the roof and were now standing beneath the strings of lights, soft music drifting on the warm night air. In any other situation, it would have been a setting ripe for seduction. But the dance lessons had killed any sense of romance.

"Maybe I just shouldn't venture near the dance floor," he finally said.

"I'm not giving up. Think about how you move in bed," Malin explained.

"If I do that, they'll toss me out on the street."

Malin groaned, shaking her head. "All right, let's

try this." She grabbed his hips and yanked him against her body. "Stay close. Our hips need to move together."

As she began to move against him, she softly counted to the music. "Sway with it. Just a little more. Think about taking my clothes off. About running your hands over my naked body. But just keep moving. Right, left, right, left."

"Am I supposed to get aroused?" Thom asked.

"No, but we'll just chalk that up to rookie inexperience. Now slip this arm around my waist and pull me a little closer. Now it's full-body contact. One, two, three, one, two, three. Let the music move you. Don't worry about counting."

To Thom's surprise, he actually seemed to be making some progress. "This is good," he said, running his hand over her back. His fingers found a natural spot, right above her backside, his fingers splayed wide as he directed the sway of her hips.

She'd tried to explain to him what it meant to lead, but now he felt it, how she silently ceded control and just followed his direction.

The more they moved, the easier the dance became. She rested her head against his shoulder and Thom kissed her temple. He'd never really appreciated how amazing she felt in his arms. Slender, delicate, her waist almost narrow enough to span with his hands, her breasts perfect.

Thom understood the allure of dancing. It was foreplay in slow motion. Instead of acting, he was left to anticipate, to imagine, what might happen between them.

"You're dancing," she whispered.

"Shh," he murmured. "Don't mess it up."

They continued to dance, moving seamlessly from one song to the next. But the mood was spoiled when Thom's phone rang. He recognized the ringtone as the melody he'd assigned to his agent.

"Let it go," she said.

"I can't. It's Jack Warren, my agent. He might have some news on the trade."

Malin grabbed his shirt and held tight, pulling him down into a long, languid kiss. For a moment, Thom considered ignoring the call. The odds of his agent having good news were pretty thin. But then, if it was bad news, he'd rather know now. If he'd been traded, then there wouldn't be any reason to dance with Malin at the benefit.

"I'll just be a minute," he said. He let go of her, leaving Malin to stand in the middle of their makeshift dance floor. When he got to the phone, it had already gone to voice mail. He quickly dialed Jack's number.

"Hi, it's me," he said when Jack picked up.

"Hi," Jack said. "I'm outside your place. Do you have a moment to talk?"

"Yeah," Thom said. "Sure. I'll be right down to let you in." He hung up the phone and turned to Malin. "Jack is here. He wants to talk to me." Over the last couple of days, Malin hadn't said anything about her trip to the office on Sunday. She'd claimed that there wasn't any news about his trade. But as he looked deep into her eyes, he saw the raw fear behind her calm demeanor. "What do you know?"

"Nothing solid," she said. "Just that they're getting close to working out a deal."

Thom felt a sick knot tighten in his stomach and he drew a deep breath, waiting for the wave of nausea to pass. He'd never once believed that his career wouldn't begin and end in his hometown. And now that it was all about to change, he realized how lucky he'd been.

Maybe that was the lesson he was supposed to learn. A guy never really knew how good things were until he lost everything. And it wasn't just his team and his home. It was Malin. She'd come along at a time when he'd allowed his life to drift in the wrong direction. He'd been drinking too much and partying too much. She'd shown him how empty his life had been.

"Will you come with me?"

"Of course."

Malin followed him downstairs and stood next to him, her fingers laced through his as he opened the door.

The moment Jack Warren spotted them, his gaze dropped to their joined hands. Thom could see the discomfort in his expression, but he didn't care. Jack was probably one of the only guys he knew who wouldn't spread rumors around town.

"This is new," he said as he walked past Thom.

"We're both enjoying it, so keep any negative thoughts to yourself, all right?" Thom said.

Jack walked to the dining room table and set his briefcase on top. "You're Davis Pedersen's daughter," he said to Malin. "If your father finds out about this, Thom will be on the next boat to Siberia. He'll be playing in run-down arenas with clubs that can barely keep the lights on and the ice frozen."

"I don't intend to mention this to my father," Malin said.

"I think that's wise," Jack replied.

Thom cleared his throat, and Jack glanced over at him. "You said you had some news?"

"They're negotiating with New York and Vancouver," Jack said. "They want to know if you have a preference. They said they weren't going to honor the approval clause in your contract, but the players' association stepped in and threatened a grievance."

"I have to choose between the two?" Thom asked.

Jack nodded. "They're both great teams. You could do a lot worse. New York would put you closer to home, but Vancouver is a lot like Minneapolis. And they're closer to having a championship team."

"There is another choice," Malin said. "You could say no to both."

"I wouldn't recommend that," Jack said. "Right now you have the choice of two great teams, both of which would benefit from your talents. You'd be a star in either city. They could send you to much worse places."

"But if he turned them down, it would buy us some time to change their minds," Malin said.

"I highly doubt there's much chance of that," Jack countered.

Malin shook her head. "We can't just give up."

Thom gave her hand a squeeze, then pulled her wrist up to his lips and pressed a kiss to the skin above her fingers. "How much time do I have to give them an answer?"

"A week. Maybe a little longer. But the sooner, the better. Holding out to stay with the Blizzard is a hopeless cause at this point. Listen, Thom, you've got a lot of good hockey left in you. I want to see you land somewhere you'll make a difference."

Thom reached out and clapped his agent on the shoulder. "Thanks for stopping by. I'll walk you to the door."

He left Malin standing alone at the dining room table. When he got to the door, Jack turned to him, a serious expression clouding his face. "End this," he said. "You don't want to give them a reason to run you out of town on a rail, Thom. She's a beautiful woman, but she's not worth the trouble that she can cause."

"I'm in love with her," Thom admitted.

"Get over it. It will be better for both of you. Ask yourself if she really has your best interests at heart, or her own."

Thom shut the door and leaned against it, closing his eyes as his agent's words echoed in his head. Maybe he had been living in a fantasy world, thinking that everything would work out between him and Malin. Hell, he couldn't even define what real love was. How did he know that's what he was feeling for Malin?

And she'd been cagey about her feelings toward him. She was affectionate and engaged and interested in everything about his life. But she'd made it clear she didn't want to talk about their future. Anything beyond the summer existed in a deep black void. And she'd just said to his agent that she had no intention of telling her father about their relationship. How serious could she be about him?

"Is he gone?"

Thom looked up and nodded. She held out a tumbler to him, filled with ice and water. "Do you want to talk about what he said?"

"Did you know about New York and Vancouver?"

Malin nodded. "My father mentioned it."

"Why didn't you tell me?"

"It was proprietary information. It's my duty to keep it private."

"That's bullshit," Thom said, anger creeping into his voice. "The minute you moved in here, you stopped being one of them."

"Fine. I didn't tell you because I really believed I could change his mind," Malin said. "I didn't want you to give up hope. And I didn't want to believe you'd have to leave here." She swallowed hard. "Leave me."

Thom reached out and pulled her into his arms. "Don't do that again. Don't keep secrets from me. If we have anything between us, at least we have honesty."

"I promise," Malin said.

He pressed a kiss to the top of her head. Thom was tempted to drag her off to bed, to lose himself in her body and forget all the doubts and fears that had come creeping into his head. But he needed some time to clear his head, to sort out all the choices that had to be made.

"I'm going to take a drive," he said. "I won't be long. I just want some fresh air."

"I'll come with you," Malin said.

"No, I just need to be alone. I'll be back soon, I promise. And I won't get in any trouble."

"I trust you," she said.

Thom grabbed his keys from the counter, then slipped his phone in the pocket of his shorts. "I'll see you later. We'll continue our dance lesson. I think I was finally getting the hang of it."

Malin nodded, then opened the door for him. "Later," she said.

Thom bent close and gave her a lingering kiss. "Later."

THOM DIDN'T COME HOME that night. Malin waited until 4:00 a.m., trying to convince herself that nothing was wrong. He was probably out at some bar, hanging out with old friends. He'd probably come home stumbling drunk, but Malin was determined to maintain a positive attitude and forgive him any transgressions he might have committed.

In the end, he'd done nothing more than turn his car northward and continue driving until the sun came up. He'd called from a gas station in northern Minnesota, apologizing for worrying her and telling her that he'd decided to escape for a few days to his cabin.

It had been a short conversation, no confessions of affection or claims of longing. And when he hung up, Malin felt an emptiness settle into her body, as if he'd stolen a part of her soul before leaving.

The emotions roiling inside her both frightened and surprised her. Malin had tried to keep her feelings for

Thom in perspective. She knew that unless she could save his spot on the Blizzard roster, he'd be shipped right out of her life, courtesy of her own father.

And while he was taking time to be alone, Malin was facing her own demons.

Malin stared out the windshield of her car at the imposing facade of her parents' home, located in the stately Kenwood neighborhood. It was never a home she'd lived in, as it was purchased and decorated after she'd left home for college. But it was the kind of show-case that was required for the man who owned one of the city's most successful sports franchises.

She parked the car in the circular drive, then grabbed the dress box from the backseat and walked to the front door to ring the bell. Though she could have just gone right inside, Malin knew that ringing the bell would bring the family's cook and housekeeper to the door, and she hadn't seen Dottie in ages. To her surprise, her father appeared in the doorway.

"Ah, here you are. Your mother is waiting for you on the terrace."

"Daddy! What are you doing here? It's a weekday."

"Oh, nothing special. Just slept in."

"Is everything all right? Are you all right?"

Davis Pedersen smiled. "Just fine. Fit as a fiddle," he said, nodding to himself. "Must get to work now."

He turned away from the door and headed in the di-rection of the garage. Malin closed the door and walked through the spacious entry hall to the French doors at the other end.

Peering through the wavering glass, she watched

as Lillian Cooke Pedersen poured herself a cup of tea from a china pot, then slowly stirred in a half teaspoon of sugar. She usually wore her ash-blond hair in a tidy twist, but today it was a mass of tangled ringlets, making her look much younger than her fifty-six years.

"Hello, Mama," Malin said as she stepped out onto the terrace.

"Darling! Here you are! I was wondering if you'd decided not to come."

"No, I was just running a few minutes late. I just saw Daddy. What's he doing home so late on a workday?"

Lillian smiled, then took a sip of her tea. "Your father and I have a deal. He has to spend two weekday mornings at home with me, and then I won't complain about him staying out until all hours during hockey season. It's working out quite well," she said with a coy arch of her eyebrow.

Malin sat down next to her mother, placing the box on a nearby chair, then quickly poured herself a cup of tea. If her mother was talking about sex, then she didn't want any part of the conversation. Though she knew her parents were still attracted to each other, she'd never actually thought about them having sex. And didn't intend to start now.

"Is it that difficult to imagine that we were once very hot for each other?" Lillian asked. "Because we were. Just couldn't keep our hands off each other. And this was in the seventies!"

"You've never talked that much about how you and Daddy met. Only that it was in high school."

"Your father was on the hockey team, and my girl-friends and I just thought those boys were better than rock stars. He was the captain, of course, and he had a scholarship to a great college, and though he didn't end up going, I just knew he was the guy for me."

"Daddy went to college," Malin said.

"Oh, much later. After you children were born. After high school, he played professional hockey. Much to the consternation of my parents. They did every-thing in their power to break us up. They didn't want me marrying a lowly hockey player. They wanted me to marry a doctor or a lawyer. But your father wanted to play hockey." She sighed. "Of course, he wasn't very good. We spent most of our time bouncing around the minor league teams, living in crummy apartments and existing on nothing. And then I got pregnant with your older brother, and my father said enough was enough. He offered your father a job, and Davis walked away from hockey."

"Until he bought the team," Malin said. She'd read her father's bio many times on the website, but it con-tained nothing about his days as a minor league hockey player.

"Yes, with the inheritance from my father," Lillian said. "I knew it would give him back what I'd taken away from him. It was money well spent."

"Why haven't I heard any of this before?"

"You know your father. He didn't want anyone to think of him as a failure or someone who hadn't de-served his status—least of all his children."

"So why are you telling me this now?" Malin asked.

"You're father says you're bringing a date to the hospital benefit. That you wanted to sit at our table. I suppose I was just hoping that you'd found someone who caught your interest."

Malin plucked a shortbread cookie off the china plate and munched on it, contemplating how much she actually wanted to tell her mother. Now that she'd been given the details of their past, how could they possibly object to her dating a player?

"There is a guy," she said. "We've been seeing quite a bit of each other. But it's complicated. He might have to take a transfer out of town, so our future is kind of sketchy."

"What does he do?" Lillian asked. "Maybe your father could give him a job."

Malin laughed. "I think you'd like him. He's kind of a self-made man. He didn't have a lot of breaks in life, but he hasn't let that stop him. And he's so kind and generous and funny."

"He sounds wonderful," Lillian said. "I can hardly wait to meet him."

"I do have something for you," Malin said. "When I decided to go to the banquet, I called a designer friend of mine and asked her to send me a few gowns to wear. The first one was perfect for me. But the second one was too beautiful to just send back without anyone here ever getting a chance to see it."

Malin pushed the box across the table. Her mother, a surprised smile on her face, stood to open it. The short-sleeved gown was a lovely champagne color with a bodice of bugle beads and a layered chiffon skirt.

"It's gorgeous," Lillian said, her fingers tracing over the bodice. She examined the label, then looked up at Malin. "You know her?"

"Yes. She's a very talented and generous woman. And she told me that she'd love it if you'd wear her dress."

"You had such an important job in New York," Lillian said. "A dream job. Why did you ever come back?"

"It just felt like the right time to come home," Malin said. "I have something to offer the team, and I hoped Daddy would see that. I still hope he does."

"Darling, you have always been his little girl. But as you got older, he just didn't know what to do with you. There was nothing you two had in common."

"I could have played hockey," Malin said.

"That was my fault. I wouldn't allow it. I thought it was too rough for a girl, and let's face it, you were not built for the game." She held up her hand. "Parents make the best decisions they can at the time. When you have daughters, you can let them play hockey."

"I'll remember that," Malin said softly.

There were moments in her life when she could imagine her future so clearly. A husband and children. A comfortable home. But since she'd been with Thom, that vision had become blurred. Could she be happy with less? Could she be happy without Thom?

7

THE FOUR-HOUR DRIVE back to the city became a race against the weather. Three days of sweltering temperatures had brought a line of fierce thunderstorms bearing down on the area. Thom watched them approach, lightning flashing on the horizon, as he sped toward home.

He'd made the decision to escape to his cabin quickly and without much thought to what it might mean to Malin. But at that moment, faced with deciding the rest of his career, he wasn't sure that he wanted her at his side.

There was no doubt anymore that he cared about her. Or that he might even be in love with her. But Thom had always made all his decisions with only two things in mind—his family and himself. Changing that now did not come easily. There were so many ways that it could play out. He could ask her to come with him. He could ask her to wait. He could break it off entirely and go on as he had in the past—alone. And he still had some lingering doubts about how much she truly cared for him.

Thom glanced at the clock on the dash. He'd deliberately left the cabin early enough to get home and change for the hospital benefit, but with pelting rain starting to come down, he'd been forced to take it slow.

Impatient, he reached for the radio and tuned into one of his favorite sports talk shows, hoping to find out how his favorite baseball team had done that week. But as he caught the gist of the conversation, Thom realized they were talking about him.

"He's been a core player since the moment he stepped on the ice," a caller explained. "You don't just trade away part of that core."

"It happens all the time," the host, Jay Robbins, said. "And when a star player is bringing the team down, you have to do what you have to do."

Jay's cohost, Jerry Baumer, jumped in. "There's no evidence that he's let his partying affect his play. Players should be allowed to have a personal life."

"Not when it's splashed all over the tabloids," Jay countered.

"We're going to take another call. This is Denise, from Eagan. Denise, welcome to the Jay and Jerry Show."

"Hi, guys. I just want to say that if they trade Thom Quinn, they're going to lose a lot of fans. He's always been out there, giving a hundred percent, and my son really admires him. He proves that with a little talent and a lot of hard work, you can make it as a professional hockey player. I approve of that message."

"Well, there you have it from the mom contingent," Jay said. "After we take a break, we're going to get into the Twitter war that is raging between Blizzard management and hockey fans statewide. While the team tries to defend its decision, the fans aren't having it."

Thom reached for the radio and switched to a classic rock station. He felt in his pocket for his cell phone. He'd forgotten the charger at home, so it had been dead for a few days. Not that it made a difference since there was no service at the cabin.

He'd called Malin the morning after he'd arrived at the cabin, and though she'd been glad to hear that he was all right, he could tell she'd been confused by his retreat. But he wouldn't regret leaving. It was impossible to think straight when he was around her. She colored his every thought and decision.

To say he'd missed her over the past few days would have been an understatement. He'd thought about her nearly every waking moment, and images of her teased at his dreams each night. When had she become such an essential part of his life? She was like oxygen, food and water...sunlight. When Malin wasn't with him, he felt the loss, as if his strength was slowly being sapped from his body.

The rain was coming down in sheets, and the truck suddenly started to drift as it hit deep water on the pavement. He checked the rearview mirror, then turned on his flashers, hoping to make himself more visible to the cars behind him.

His fingers tightened around the steering wheel, and he searched for the lines on the highway to guide him.

Though it was barely past 6:00 p.m., it was almost as dark as midnight.

Thom thought about the night ahead of him. He'd considered calling Malin when he got home to let her know that he'd be at the benefit as they planned. But Thom was worried that their time apart might have changed her mind. It would be much better to just show up and take his chances. He sure as hell wasn't going to miss her in that dress.

A smile curled the corners of his mouth. He'd been known to date beautiful women—the majority of them models or actresses. But they'd all shared a kind of look that left nothing in its natural state. Malin was a beauty inside and out. To him, she was the most beautiful when she was stepping out of the shower, her skin fresh and clean, her hair dripping with water.

He thought about his teammates' wives, many of them ordinary women, women Thom had never believed to be beautiful. But those guys had done it right. They'd found beauty that wasn't just floating on the surface. It ran deep, and it would last a lifetime.

He squinted through the rain and was relieved to see the first exit for the city was only eight miles away. By his calculations, he was twenty minutes from home. He could still grab a quick shower, get dressed and make it to the dinner before the speeches began.

As if the fates were aware of his important plans, the rain suddenly stopped, and the skies in the west began to clear. He opened the window and took a deep breath of the cool, fresh air. He felt a familiar sense of anticipation inside of him, an excitement for what the evening might hold. Usually this came before an important game, but tonight somehow seemed even more important.

He'd made the decision to take the New York trade. Though Vancouver was a better team, he preferred to move to a place that had the most direct flights to Minneapolis. He would be closer to his brothers, and though he wasn't sure he and Malin would have a future past the beginning of the season, Thom preferred to believe that they would.

He also knew that Malin had spent the first part of her career working in Manhattan. She'd loved the city, and if she loved him, she might consider moving back. It wasn't beyond the realm of possibility.

By the time he pulled up in front of the curb of his house, the sun was drifting down to the horizon. He searched the street for Malin's car and felt a small sliver of disappointment when he realized she wasn't there. He hadn't expected her to stay, but a tiny part of him had hoped that she would.

When he got inside, Thom tossed his keys on the counter and slowly walked through the first floor. There was no trace of her left beyond the faint scent of her perfume in the air. The bed was made, the covers smooth. Had she even stayed in his house?

He stepped inside the bathroom and ran his hand along the edge of the marble counter. Over the few weeks that they were together, he'd enjoyed the mess of beauty products that had littered the surface. It was all gone, except the bottles and jars of skin care products that she'd given him after their day at the spa.

He picked up the exfoliating cream and the new shaving supplies, then set them in front of him. The stubble of his beard was thick with three days' growth. Thom reached for the hem of his T-shirt and pulled it over his head, then stripped out of his cargo shorts.

In less than an hour, he'd see Malin. He'd tell her about his decision and then he'd lay it all on the line. He'd confess how much she meant to him and exactly how he wanted their future together to begin.

And if she refused, he'd move on with his life and try to forget that he'd ever touched her…or kissed her… or lay beside her in his bed. He would pretend that the past few weeks had never happened and Malin Pedersen had never spoken to him that day in the conference room.

THE BALLROOM AT the Franklin Hotel was decorated in a veil of tiny white lights and leafless trees, their branches and trunks painted white. Malin had been to the annual benefit before, but this time around, her mother had served on the decorations committee.

"Mama, it's stunning," she said, giving Lillian a quick hug. "The prettiest ever."

"Look how the lights reflect off the crystal and silver," Lillian said, clapping her hands beneath her chin. "I know it's silly, but isn't it all right to be a little silly over a good cause?"

"Of course it is," Malin said.

"Now, then, where is this date of yours?"

Malin swallowed hard and pasted a smile on her face. Truth be told, her "date" was somewhere close to the Canadian border, living in a cabin with no electricity or running water. "Oh, didn't I tell you? He called and said he wouldn't be able to come. He had an emergency at the hospital."

"He's a doctor?" Lillian asked.

"No," Malin said. "I—I mean, yes. He's—he's an oncologist."

"Hmm. Where did I get the impression that he was a surgeon?"

Malin desperately searched around the room for someone who might capture her mother's attention. "I don't know, Mama, but—oh, look there. Mrs. Jenkins is walking with a cane. I hope she hasn't injured herself. We should go over and say hello."

When her mother was safely delivered to another conversation, Malin headed over to the table that held the seating cards. She found Natalie there and smiled as she approached. "Hello," she said. "Are you handling the seating arrangements?"

"Just until Mrs. Farner gets back."

Malin looked for her name and then found the card for her guest. She held it out to Natalie. "I'm afraid my guest can't make it tonight. You can assign someone else to our table if necessary."

"All right. I think everyone has a place for now, but I'm sure there might be a few strays who wander in."

"Table seven," Malin said, holding up her card. "I'll see you there."

Malin strolled around the ballroom, stopping to chat with acquaintances of her parents, people connected to the team and occasionally friends she could call her own. Nearly every woman she met had something to say about her dress, and by the time she sat down for dinner, she felt quite beautiful.

But as her parents and the other guests took their places at the table, Malin was feeling much less festive. She couldn't help but wonder how much of that had to do with Thom's absence.

It was probably for the best that he hadn't come, she mused. Putting him and her father in the same room was like tossing gasoline and lit matches into the same barrel.

"I see everyone is here."

The guests at the table turned to find Betsy Farner, one of her mother's dear friends, standing next to the empty chair.

"Lillian, since you have a vacant spot at your table, I wonder if I might seat someone here. We had a spot for him at table thirteen, but then Bebe Smithfield brought an extra guest. I'm sure you all know Thom Quinn. He's been a very good friend to the hospital."

Thom stepped out from behind Betsy, and his gaze immediately met Malin's. At first she wasn't sure what to say, but one look at her father's increasingly purple face was all it took for her to come up with something fast. "Thom! How nice to see you again."

The empty chair was right next to her father's, and since she was determined to keep the peace as best she could, she scrambled to come up with an alternate plan. "Mama, why don't you sit in that spot, and we'll put Thom right here where I'm sitting." Malin slipped into her mother's abandoned spot, putting herself squarely between the two men in her life.

"There, that will work."

Lillian frowned as her gaze shifted between Malin and the new guest.

"Sorry to be a bother," Thom said. "I guess they didn't get my RSVP."

"Lucky for us that your date couldn't make it, Malin," her mother said. "Now we have the charming Mr. Quinn for company." She turned to her husband and gave him a stern look. "And there will be no talk about hockey at this table."

The hour between the beginning and end of dinner service passed at a grinding pace. Malin tried to maintain a cheerful attitude without revealing a clue about her real feelings for Thom. He, on the other hand, seemed to be determined to charm every woman at the table.

She was beginning to wonder if he was going to ignore her completely when Malin felt his leg brush up against hers beneath the cover of the linen tablecloth. Her breath caught at the powerful current that raced through her body.

She stretched her foot out, then slipped out of her shoe. Malin found the cuff of his trousers and wriggled her toes up inside until she touched bare skin. When Thom cleared his throat, she knew the game had begun.

Thom's hand found the slit in her skirt and he smoothed his palm over her thigh, moving higher and higher.

The dress didn't allow for underwear, and Malin

had to hold back a laugh when Thom discovered that fact on his own. For a moment, his hand froze, and he stole a glance over at her.

Malin dropped her napkin next to her plate. "If you'll excuse me, I'm going to go to the ladies' room."

Natalie jumped up. "I'll go with you."

The two of them walked through the crowd, dodging the wait staff that had begun to clear the dinner plates and bring out dessert. When they got out to the hallway, Natalie turned to her. "Gosh, that dress is just amazing, Malin. Where did you get it?"

"From a designer friend in New York," Malin said. "I used to work in the fashion industry before I came back home to work for the club."

"I heard that. Well, it's no wonder Thom Quinn can't keep his eyes off you."

Malin stopped short. "What do you mean?"

"Haven't you noticed?"

"No. He's paying attention to all the women. He's very charming."

"I can't believe you're so oblivious. Every time you say anything, he watches you with this look of rapture on his face." Natalie frowned, then studied Malin for a shrewd moment. "Wait...are you two...? Is there something— Is that why you wanted to invite him to the benefit?" She gasped. "Do you have a crush on him?" Natalie clapped her hands gleefully. "And he has a crush on you? Oh, this is just too—"

"Stop," Malin said. "I don't have a crush on Thom Quinn. And he doesn't have a crush on me."

Natalie stared over Malin's left shoulder. "Well, I

guess you should probably tell him that, because he's heading this way, and I don't think he's coming to talk to me."

Malin turned just in time for Thom to catch her hand as he walked by. "Come on," he said. "We need to talk."

"Talk?" Malin asked, trailing after him. "What could we possibly have to talk about?"

"Go for it!" Natalie called.

Thom took a quick right and led her down another hallway, this one lined with smaller conference rooms. He tested each door as they passed by, and when he found one open, he drew her inside. The room was dark except for the red light glowing from the exit sign above the door.

Malin didn't have a chance to speak. The moment the door was closed, he pulled her into a deep and powerful kiss. As his mouth ravished hers, his hands skimmed over her body, pressing her back against the door until his hips pinned hers and she couldn't escape.

The surge of desire was so sudden that it worked like a drug on her mind, making her giddy and weak all at once. She returned the kiss, her tongue probing at his until he groaned softly.

"God, I missed you," he murmured against her damp lips.

"Why did you leave?" Malin asked. "I was afraid you'd never come back."

"Did you really think I was going to miss seeing you in this dress? You look…breathtaking."

"That's funny," she said. "Right now, I'm the one who can't breathe."

"Let's get out of here," he whispered. "As much as I love that dress, I'd like to get rid of it as soon as possible."

"We can't leave," she said. "Not yet."

His hand slid up her torso to cup her breast. He teased at her nipple through the thin fabric. The rough surface of the beaded bodice created a delicious friction, and her nipple grew hard.

Thom's lips moved from her mouth to her neck and then trailed lower, into the deep V of the dress's neckline. When he knelt in front of her, Malin wasn't sure where he was going—until he slipped his hands into the slit of the skirt and gently drew it up along her thighs.

He moved his hand between her legs, gently forcing them apart. Then he bent close and ran his tongue along the moist slit, parting the soft folds of flesh with his fingers.

Malin's knees went weak as a wave of sensation poured over her. She braced her hands on his shoulders for balance, her fingertips digging into the fine fabric of his tux jacket. Every nerve in her body was alive, snapping with excitement as the orgasm began to build inside her.

He brought her to the edge once and then again. Malin whispered her need, begging him to give her release from his delicious torment. Finally, he relented and the orgasm hit her in a powerful series of spasms.

A groan tore from her throat as she writhed against the door. She gently pushed him away when she couldn't handle it anymore. Malin gasped for breath, her heart slamming against the inside of her chest, her pulse pounding.

Thom sat back on his heels as Malin slowly sank to the floor. She reached out and smoothed her hand over his cheek. A smile touched the corners of her mouth. "Did you exfoliate?" she asked.

Thom chuckled, then turned and kissed the palm of her hand. "I did. And I used that new shaving cream and razor, too."

"You're very handsome," she said.

"Look at you. I've gotta bring some game if we're going to take a spin around the dance floor."

"We're going to dance?" Malin asked. "I'm not sure I can even walk."

"Come on," Thom said. He stood up and held out his hand. "If you don't want to leave yet, we'd better get back before they wonder where we are."

Malin stood up beside him, smoothing her hands over her dress. "You should go. Grab a few drinks on your way in as if you went to the bar. And I'll come in a few minutes later. I'll say I met an old friend in the hall and we got carried away talking."

"And then I can ask you to dance?"

Malin smiled. "The band isn't going to start for a while. But I'll save my first dance for you."

"And when can we leave?"

"We'll figure that out a bit later. Just go. I'll see you in a few minutes."

Thom gave her a quick kiss, nuzzling her cheek before stepping back out into the hall. When he was gone, Malin drew a ragged breath. How would she look when she went back into the ballroom? Would anyone be able to tell that she'd just been well-pleasured by a man? Would they suspect she was with Thom? Natalie would, for sure. Hopefully the woman would be smart enough to keep her suspicions to herself.

Malin rushed to the bathroom and found a spot in front of the mirror. To her great relief, she appeared perfectly normal. Her hair was a bit mussed, but she'd paid the stylist to make it look as if she'd just crawled out of bed anyway.

She grabbed her purse and hurried back to the ballroom. But when she got to the table, Natalie was the only one still seated.

"Where did everyone go?" Malin asked.

"Your father and mother are over there," she said, pointing, "talking to the mayor. The rest of them have wandered off. And I suppose you'd know as well as anyone where Thom Quinn is."

"Please, don't say anything about what you saw in the hallway."

"What did I see?" Natalie asked.

Malin took a deep breath. "You saw two people trying to figure out how they really feel about each other. What's going on between us is very complicated."

"You're telling me!" Natalie said. "If looks could kill, your father would be in jail for murder right now, and we'd be singing hymns at Thom Quinn's funeral."

"There you go," Malin said. "Complicated."

"I'll keep your secret," the other woman said. "But I will say this. I think you two would be great together. I hope it works out."

Malin smiled. "Me, too. And it's past time I had a talk with my father. When Thom returns to the table, have him wait here. I'll be right back."

It was as good an opportunity as any, Malin thought to herself as she walked through the crowd. When she reached her father and mother, she stood silently and listened to their conversation. Though her father had voted for another mayoral candidate, he seemed to be quite happy to talk hockey with this one.

She waited for a break in the conversation. "Daddy, could I speak with you for a quick moment?"

"Malin, if this is about—"

She took his arm. "There's a bench against the wall. Why don't we sit down. I promise, it won't take long."

Davis Pedersen followed her, but when they reached the bench, he refused to sit down. "What is it? Are you going to apologize to me for seating Quinn at our table? That was a clever trick."

"I didn't have anything to do with that," Malin said.

"Right," Davis said. "Give me a little credit."

"Daddy, do you love me?"

The question seemed to take him by surprise. "What is this about?"

"Do you? It's a simple question. Yes or no. Do you love me?"

"Of course I do. You're my daughter."

"And do you remember when I was little, how we used to sit at the little table in my playroom and we'd have tea? And you'd call me your princess and tell me that you'd grant me any wish that I wanted. All I had to do was ask."

"I remember," Davis said with a wistful smile. "I never thought you would ask."

"Well, now I'm going to ask for that wish. I want you to stop the trade negotiations for Thom Quinn. I—I need you to stop."

"Linny, we've discussed this. It's a business decision."

"Not for me," Malin said. "I—I think I might be... in love. With him. With Thom Quinn."

Her father laughed. "The man is charming, but one dinner conversation is not enough for me to believe that—"

"We've been seeing each other," Malin said. "Remember you asked me to watch him? Well, it became a bit more than that. We've been together since that day in the conference room. Believe me, Daddy, I never saw this coming. But I can't deny it any longer. Please, for my sake, keep Thom with the club."

"And you think he feels the same way about you?"

"I hope he does," Malin said.

Her father shook his head. "If he does care for you, why did I get a call from Steve McCrory just a few minutes before we stepped in for dinner, letting me know that Quinn chose New York?"

The news stole the breath from her body. She opened her mouth to speak but nothing came out. So she just shook her head, turned and walked away from her father.

She glanced over at the table and saw Thom sitting with Natalie. If she wanted answers, then she'd have to go directly to the source.

"THERE SHE IS," Thom said, rising from his spot at the table. "Excuse me for a moment."

Natalie took a sip of her wine and gave him a little wave. "Take all the time you need."

They met in the middle of a crowd, and Thom rested his hand on the small Malin's back as they spoke. It was an innocent way to touch her, a gesture that would attract no curiosity.

"The band is warming up," he said. "And you promised me the first dance."

"I'm really not in the mood for dancing. I think I'm going to head home."

Thom stared down at her, trying to read the expression on her face. She wasn't angry, but then she didn't appear to be very happy, either. "You're going to let all those painful dance lessons you gave me go to waste?"

"My father said you've agreed to the trade to New York. When were you going to tell me?"

Thom cursed inwardly. His agent had caught him right before he'd left for the benefit and had been determined to get an answer. Though Malin still refused to accept the reality of his situation, a week at the cabin had clarified his own thoughts. He had a choice and he'd made it.

"Can't we discuss this later?" Thom asked.

"*Now* you want to discuss it? After you've made your decision?"

He drew a deep breath. "It was my decision to make."

"But you didn't give it enough time. You could have refused. You have a no-trade clause."

"That doesn't mean they can't trade me," he said. "If I refuse, they could bench me or send me down to the farm team. I need to finish out the next two years of this contract, and it's better to play where I want to play. And that's New York."

"You don't understand what's been going on. While you were gone, there's been so much fan and media support for you. Believe me, the guys in the main office are rethinking their decision. The backlash is growing."

"I just wanted it to be settled," he said. "And now that it is, we can make some decisions of our own." He looked up and noticed guests moving toward the dance floor. "Come on, let's dance."

She pulled out of his grip. "I don't want to dance."

"Sure you do. You've been anticipating this all week, and so have I."

Malin backed away from him, bumping into an elderly couple as she tried to retreat. "I have to go. I'll talk to you later."

"Come on, Malin. You knew this was coming. There was no way your father would change his mind."

"You gave up on me. I would never have given up on you." She turned and hurried out of the ballroom, leaving Thom standing at the edge of the dance floor, alone. Thom ran his fingers through his short-cropped hair, cursing softly.

As his gaze scanned the dance floor, Thom spotted Malin's parents, who were gliding gracefully to the strains of the big band tune. Thom strode back to the table and held out his hand to Natalie. "Would you like to dance?"

"Me?" Natalie asked, looking over her shoulder as if he were talking to someone else. "You want to dance with me?"

"Come on. It'll be fun."

Thom led Natalie onto the floor. It took a few attempts before he found the rhythm and began to move to the music. And he had to change some of Malin's rules about what he could and couldn't touch, since he was dancing with a complete stranger. But that didn't matter. He had a purpose in mind.

When they danced close to Malin's parents, he stopped and nodded at them both. "Switch partners?"

Lillian's eyes lit up. "I would love to dance with you, Mr. Quinn. Unless you had my husband in mind."

"I'll start with you, Mrs. Pedersen."

Lillian switched places with Natalie, and Davis Pedersen reluctantly began to dance with the pretty brunette. Thom was feeling confident about his dancing skills, but it was clear Lillian was much more adept.

"Just relax," she said. "And try to avoid my toes.'

"I don't do much dancing in my line of work," he said.

"Well, you do possess a fair amount of grace on the ice. There's not a whole lot of difference between skating and dancing." She paused. "So, why have you dragged me away from my husband? I'm guessing you'd like to discuss my daughter?"

"Malin?"

"That's the only daughter I have. She's the one you've been watching all night long. I assume you've developed some kind of crush on her."

"It's more than just that, Mrs. Pedersen."

"You'd better call me Lillian. Because I think you're about to tell me that you're in love with my daughter."

Thom chuckled softly. "You got that from the way I was looking at her over the dinner table?"

"That and a conversation I had with her a few days ago. You were supposed to be her date tonight. And for some reason, you didn't show up on time. There was a little hanky-panky going on under the table. Don't worry, I'm the only one who noticed. And then you two disappeared." Lillian peered over Thom's shoulder. "Did she leave?"

"We had a disagreement," Thom said.

"She can be stubborn."

"That's what I like about her," Thom said. "She isn't afraid to say what's on her mind. She's so honest and kind, and I can almost imagine spending my entire life with her. But…"

"Ah, there's always a problem, isn't there?"

"I know your husband would disapprove. I suspect you would, too. That's not going to stop me, but it will make things more difficult."

Lillian shook her head. "I don't disapprove. And whether her father does or not isn't relevant. You two need to work this out on your own. And if you belong together, everything will work out in the end." She patted him on the shoulder. "Now, I have just one question for you. Why are you here telling me how you feel instead of telling my daughter?"

"You're right," he said. "I should go. I have a lot of explaining to do." He leaned close and kissed her cheek. Lillian Pedersen was a beautiful woman, inside and out. It was easy to see why her marriage had lasted so long.

He returned Lillian to her husband, ignoring the glower that Davis Pedersen gave him. "Mr. Pedersen, I want you to know that my intentions toward your daughter are entirely honorable. I care for her a great deal, and though I'm aware how you feel about me, I'm going to make it my job to prove you wrong. I'm the right guy for her."

"You'll forgive me if I don't believe you," Davis said. "And I plan to do everything in my power to stop you."

"Malin is a wonderful woman, and I'd expect nothing less." With that, he grabbed Natalie's arm and strode off the dance floor.

"That was so romantic," Natalie said. "It was like a movie and you were the hero. Fighting for your woman. Did you have that all planned? I mean, what you were going to say? If some guy ever said that about me to my parents, they'd lock him up in the basement and throw away the key so he wouldn't be able to leave until he married me."

Thom glanced down at Natalie, and she snapped her mouth shut. "Sorry. That sounded really weird, didn't it? My parents have been pretty anxious for me to settle down. And they wouldn't lock him in the basement. Maybe the garage, but not the basement."

"I have to go after Malin. Do you need a ride home?" he asked.

"No, I brought my own car. Thanks anyway. I hope

everything works out for you two. There have been lots of stories about you floating around the office, but now that I've met you, I don't believe any of them. You're a nice guy, Thom."

Thom leaned in and gave Natalie a quick peck on the cheek. "I'll see you, Natalie."

"If you have any brothers, bring them around," she called after him.

As Thom strode through the hotel lobby and headed toward the parking garage, he reached into his pocket for his cell phone. He'd managed to put a small charge on it during his shower, but it was already losing power. He found Malin's number and dialed it, then waited for her to answer.

When she didn't, Thom cursed softly. Knowing Malin, she wasn't going to make this easy. She felt betrayed, angry, blindsided. He'd made a decision that impacted both of them and hadn't involved her.

And maybe she was right. Maybe he should have waited a little longer. After all, he could dig his heels in and stay with the Blizzard. If management wanted to make him suffer, they'd plant him on the bench or send him down. His hockey career would be over.

Thom thought about that possibility, turning it over in his mind. He wasn't ready to quit. Hell, he was at the top of his game. But there were a few positives to retirement. He and Malin could begin their lives together immediately. They'd never have to spend a day apart. There would be no road trips, no training camps, no distractions from their relationship. Though there was still twelve million left on his two-year contract, he'd been careful and invested wisely. Still, he'd always planned his financial future for one person. A wife and children changed things.

He could always back out of the trade. Since it was a weekend and he'd made his decision only a few hours ago, there could be a chance to retract it. Thom scrolled through his address book and dialed his agent's number. Jack picked up after just one ring.

"Hi, Jack. We need to talk about this trade deal. Is it too late to change my mind?"

8

MALIN STOOD ON THE roof of the firehouse, still dressed in the designer gown, though her shoes lay discarded beside the chaise. She'd slid the privacy fence aside to reveal a nighttime view of downtown St. Paul.

The rain earlier in the evening had left the plants glistening with droplets that sparkled beneath the strings of lights. It was nearly as beautiful as the ballroom, and yet Malin didn't feel very romantic.

Everything seemed to be falling apart. Malin had expected some bumps in the road with Thom, and she thought she'd prepared herself to handle the emotions that followed falling for him. But she'd never anticipated the capacity Thom had to hurt her.

He'd made the decision to leave, to take the job in New York, without even discussing it with her. And though Malin had never expected to get a vote in his decision, she'd thought he'd at least ask her opinion.

"What would you have said?" she murmured to herself.

Malin groaned, burying her face in her hands. She

would have urged him to stay and fight. To believe in her power to work it all out. To believe in a future for the two of them.

There was no future if he moved to New York—at least, not the kind of future she'd started to envision. They'd see each other whenever his schedule permitted or when she flew in to watch him play. Their time together would always be limited. A day, maybe two.

In the summer, he'd come home and they'd enjoy a real relationship. And so it would go for the next two or three or five years, their lives on hold.

Malin tipped her head back, closed her eyes and drew a deep breath. She was being selfish, focusing only on her needs and not Thom's. After all, this was his career. He'd been playing professional hockey much longer than she'd been in his life. She had no right to force his hand.

If he decided to go to New York, then she had to respect his choice. It didn't mean that he didn't love her. It didn't mean that there'd be no future for the two of them. It just meant that he wanted to continue playing the game he'd been born to play.

Malin walked over to the chaise. She grabbed a blanket draped over the back and wrapped it around herself, then curled up among the soft pillows. A warm breeze teased at the tendrils of hair around her face as she closed her eyes.

Exhaustion dragged her toward sleep. Malin wanted to let go, to put the doubts and regrets aside for just a few hours and clear her mind. She felt herself drifting…drifting…

Malin opened her eyes to the sound of his voice calling her name. She sat up, rubbing her eyes. Thom stood at the end of the chaise. "I've been looking all over for you. Your house, the office, your parents' place."

"I've been here, waiting for you," she said.

"I tried calling."

"I left my purse in the car."

Thom sat down beside her on the chaise, then held his arms out. Malin fought the urge to fall into his embrace, but in the end she needed to feel his warm arms around her body. She snuggled against him, resting her head on his chest. "I'm sorry," she said. "I had absolutely no right. It's your life, and you have to make your own decisions."

"And I was just thinking the opposite. Maybe you should make the decision for me."

She pressed her hand against his chest, sitting up until she could look into his eyes. "What? Why would you let me do that?"

"Because, in the end, I will be happy no matter what you choose. But you can't be happy with whatever I choose. And I want you to be happy."

"No!" Malin said, shaking her head.

"Just listen, and then you can scold me. The way I see it, we have several good choices. One—I can stay. I risk not playing or the humiliation of being sent down to the farm team, but I really don't think they'll pay me millions to do nothing."

"What are the other options?" Malin asked.

"Two—I can retire. Just drop the stick and walk away. Three—I can go to New York and we can attempt a long-distance relationship during the season and be together in the summer. And four—I can go to New York and you can come with me."

Malin had never considered the fourth option. "There is one more. Five—we could just go our separate ways."

He studied her for a long time, his gaze fixed on her lips. Malin thought he was about to kiss her, and she ached for the feel of his lips on hers. But for now, she waited, wondering how he would react.

"Could you do that?" he asked. "Just forget everything that's happened between us and go on with your life?"

"When this started, that's exactly what I had planned to do. And so did you. This wasn't meant to last. Remember?"

He nodded. "I do."

"When did it change? When did we exchange an affair with a definite end date for something endless?"

Thom pulled her close and pressed a kiss to her forehead. Such a simple and sweet gesture, Malin thought. And yet it was filled with emotion and affection, so much that it seemed to sustain her. Could she live without him? Was it possible?

"I called my agent. I told him that I was rethinking New York. He's going to see if it's possible to back out."

"Thank you, but maybe you should go," Malin said. "My father is not your biggest fan. And if you stay and we're together, he'll make your life miserable. He'll do everything possible to punish you."

"I deserve to be punished," Thom said. "I screwed

up. I put myself in bad situations, and now I'm going to have to pay the price for being The Beast."

"You know what I wish we could do?" Malin asked. "I wish we had a pause button that we could push. Then we wouldn't have to make any decisions. We could just live our lives in the present and enjoy each other the way we always have."

Thom rolled off the chaise and held out his hand to her. "I never got that dance. You're still wearing the dress. Will you dance with me, Malin?"

She tossed the blanket aside and stood. He placed his hand on the small of her back and drew her close, capturing her fingers in his palm. To her surprise, he fell easily into a rhythm even though there was no music playing.

"I used to think that I had my whole life figured out," he said. "But I'm not sure of anything anymore."

"Is that a bad thing?"

He shook his head. "No. It's just a bit unsettling."

"I'll make you a deal," Malin said. "Why don't we spend the next week trying not to think about the future. We'll just have fun. And at the end of the week, we'll decide. If we can't, we'll put it off another week. And another, if that's not enough."

"All right," he said. "One week. But we can't put off our responsibilities indefinitely. If there's one thing I've learned in the last two weeks, it's that."

Malin sighed. She didn't want to make a decision. In truth, all she had to do was wait. At some point, the decision would be made for them.

Thom ran his hands over her body, and Malin felt

a shiver skitter through her. She reached for the side zipper on the dress and drew it down. Then, shrugging her shoulders, Malin let the material slip down her body and puddle at her feet.

Thom laughed, then opened the front of his tux and let his jacket fall to the floor. Then he reached into his pocket and took out his phone, holding it up as if to take a photo of her.

"Don't you dare," she said.

"It's just for private consumption," he said.

"Said the last person who accidentally posted a nude selfie on the internet."

"Come on," he said. "I promise, I'll toss them out right away."

Malin grabbed the phone from him and shook her head. "It's a hard-and-fast rule. No naked pictures. Ever." She held the camera up and smiled. "Undo the studs on your shirt. Just the top three."

He'd already unraveled his bow tie, and it was hanging around his neck. "All right. Now put your hands on your waist." Malin focused in on Thom's chest, tan beneath the pure white of his pleated shirt. The flash illuminated his body in the dim light, and she smiled when the picture appeared.

"There," she said. "That's sexy. Post that on Twitter. And mention the benefit."

Malin picked up her gown and started toward the stairway door. "Don't you dare take a photo of me," she warned.

"Where are you going?"

"To bed." She headed down the stairs and a few

seconds later, she heard Thom behind her. He caught up with her in the workout room, slipping his hands around her waist and picking her up off her feet. He wrapped her legs around his waist and carried her down to the ground floor.

As they walked past the kitchen, the front doorbell rang. Thom groaned softly. "Did you invite someone over?"

"No," Malin said. "Did you?"

"No," Thom said. "It's probably Charlie or one of the other neighborhood kids. They like to play roller hockey late at night in the summer. They probably want me to join in."

"I'll meet you in the bedroom," Malin said.

She found a hanger in his closet and carefully took care of her borrowed gown. Then she went into the bathroom, brushed her hair and brushed her teeth.

They'd been apart for far too long. It would be good to feel his naked body next to hers in bed.

Was it wrong to grow fond of these simple things? Or should that be left to people who were married or enjoyed long, long relationships? She and Thom had been casual lovers, never meant to last.

As the minutes passed by, Malin wondered what was keeping Thom. She grabbed a blanket from the end of the bed and wrapped it around her body. As she walked out to the kitchen, Malin heard voices. Curious, she followed the sound. When she came around a corner, she saw Thom standing near the open front door, caught up in a kiss with a beautiful brunette.

They didn't notice her at first, not until she cleared

her throat. The pair stepped away from each other and Malin could see embarrassment written all over Thom's face. The woman, however, didn't appear to be bothered at all.

"Hello," she said.

Malin was startled by her greeting. "Hello."

Thom looked back and forth between the two of them. "Jennifer, this is Malin. Malin, meet Jennifer."

"Malin? What an odd name. It's a pleasure to meet you. I'm an old friend of Thom's. Not old but, well, you know." She glanced at Thom, a bright smile on her face. "So, threesome tonight?"

Malin gasped. Threesome? "I—I'll just leave you to your guest," she finally said. She spun on her heel and hurried back to the bedroom. When she was safely in the room, she locked the door, then sat down in the middle of the bed to wait.

It wasn't long before Thom was outside, rapping on the door.

"Malin. Come on, baby, let me in. I can explain."

"Is your little friend with you?" Malin asked.

"No, she left. Can I come in? I don't like shouting."

"Liar! You shout all the time on the ice. You're a liar. What else haven't you told me?"

"Nothing. That girl was part of my past, I swear."

Malin crawled off the bed and unlocked the door. Thom came in, but she pointed at the wall. "Stand right there. Don't some any closer. Now explain. Who was that woman?"

"She's a friend. We used to have this…regular… appointment."

"She's a hooker?" Malin asked.

"No, she's a pharmaceutical sales rep from Des Moines. Her business brings her here once a month and when that happens, she drops by."

"When was the last time she 'dropped by'?"

Thom thought about his answer for a moment. "A few days before you and I met in the office."

"And when she said 'threesome,' can I assume you've done that before?"

"Do you want the truth?" Thom asked. "Or should I tell you what you want to hear?"

Malin groaned, pitching forward on the bed and burying her face in the covers. "I need a while to digest this," Malin said. "You should find another place to sleep tonight."

"All right," he said. "I'll crash on the sofa. But I want you to know that Tommy the Beast is the guy who slept with that woman and who engaged in a few threesomes. I'm not Tommy the Beast anymore. And that's because of you." He took a few steps toward her, then snatched a pillow from the bed. "I just need a pillow."

A few seconds later, he left the bedroom and Malin was alone again. She drew a ragged breath. This revelation wasn't all that unexpected. She'd heard rumors about his sexploits. The issue was whether she really trusted him. Could she trust him to involve her in making big decisions? Could she trust him with his former girlfriends? Could she trust that he had really changed?

"Malin?"

"Yes?"

"Would it make a difference if I told you that I loved you?"

Malin groaned again. "Go away. I'll figure this out tomorrow."

THOM PACED BACK and forth in front of his bedroom door, listening for some proof of life inside. He'd spent most of the night tossing and turning on the leather sofa, rewinding their conversation.

It wasn't just what they'd said to each other. Lately everything had grown so serious. He'd disappointed her not once but several times, and when that happened, he saw it on her face. That beautiful face. It killed him to be the cause of her distress or sadness.

And he seemed to be messing up a lot lately. Hell, it wasn't like he had a damn roadmap, laying out all of love's twists and turns, warning him of the hazards ahead. He'd grown up without any role models.

And then there was the biggest blunder of all—choosing that moment to tell her he loved her. It was a desperation play, one of those shots that had no hope of going in. But it was the truth.

He groaned and pressed his fingertips to his temples. "What the hell was I thinking?" How was she supposed to take him seriously after all that business with Jennifer? Sure, he'd lived a pretty wild life. A lot of guys had. That came with the job. Crowds of warm and willing women.

Thom had never regretted the way he'd lived his life—until now. Hell, he'd never expected to be judged for his choices. But he knew that Malin's reaction tonight to his sexual adventures would be just the first in a long line of revelations and reactions. He'd thought that she accepted the true Thom Quinn, but had she? Or was the rejection still coming?

After a sleepless night, he'd finally made a decision. He'd weighed all his options and examined all the angles. Now that he was sure, Thom wanted to share his plan with Malin.

He pressed his ear to the bedroom door. It was already half past nine. Malin was usually awake by eight and never slept past nine. Thom reached up to rap on the door, but before he touched the wood, the door swung open.

Malin looked at him, startled. "What are you doing?"

"Waiting for you."

She strode toward the kitchen, dressed in one of his team T-shirts.

"Did you sleep well?" he asked.

"Fine," Malin said. "Have you seen my tablet? I want to check if anyone posted photos from the benefit last night."

"It's on the counter. I plugged it in last night to charge. It should be good."

Malin grabbed the iPad and started back toward the bedroom. When she moved to close the door, Thom thrust out his arm to stop her. "Come on, Malin, don't do this. We need to talk."

"Do you have something else you want to tell me? Some new scandalous behavior that will make me blush?"

"All right, let's start there. You knew I wasn't an angel when you met me. And if you're going to get mad every time you learn about something or someone in my past, then you're pretty much going to be mad at me for the rest of my life."

"I'm not mad at you," Malin said, defeat in her eyes.

Thom grabbed her hand and pulled her along into the bathroom. He set her in front of the mirror, watching her reflection over her shoulder. "Look at that face."

She reached up and touched her cheek. "What?" Malin searched her face for some mark or flaw.

"I did that to you. You have a beautiful face and a radiant smile. Then I come along and take the fire out of your eyes."

"I know all that happened in the past. But you've promised me that you've changed, that you're not going to continue that kind of behavior. So it would be unfair for me to be angry at you."

"That's easy to say," he said. "But eventually some woman will sell her story or some photo will show up on social media, and these doubts you have will come rushing back."

She turned away from the mirror and sat down on the bed, flipping through screens on her tablet. Thom sat across from her, watching her expression.

"Ah, here. I was hoping the hospital would post something on their Twitter account. Here's me in my dress. And my mom. Gosh, she looks beautiful. I should send this to her."

Malin continued to search, then stopped again.

"'Hockey pro Thom Quinn dances with new girlfriend Natalie Monroe.'"

"You see? You can't believe everything you read on Twitter," he said.

"This is good. I mean, it's not true, but you two look great together. And she's gazing up at you like she adores you."

"But she's not my girlfriend."

Malin drew a deep breath. "I've been thinking about that, and I—"

Thom reached out and pressed his finger to her lips. "Don't say it. If you say it, you can't take it back."

"Like what you said last night?"

Thom groaned. He'd hoped she might not have heard him or that she'd forgotten. "That just kind of popped out."

"Did you mean it?"

His gaze met hers. "I did. Hell, I don't know what love between two people is, Malin. I've never really seen it, so I couldn't tell you. But I know that being with you is the best damn feeling I've ever experienced. And being without you is the worst. At the same time, I have to admit that this whole thing scares the crap out of me."

"Why?"

"I just don't know if I can be that guy. The one who makes all your dreams come true." He drew a long, deep breath. "I've decided to go ahead with the New York trade. The way I see it, it will give us some time to figure this whole thing out. I'll be back for the summer. You'll come to visit. We'll meet on the road. And you can continue to work for the team."

"You've figured it all out without me," Malin said. "Again."

"I don't want to disappoint you," he murmured. "It would kill me if I wrecked your life the way my father wrecked my mother's."

"I wouldn't let you do that," Malin said.

"Maybe not. But until I know for sure, I'm not willing to risk your happiness."

Malin took his hands and gave them a squeeze. When she looked up at him, there were tears in her eyes. "This doesn't make me happy. The thought of being without you. But the truth is, I'm not sure I completely trust you."

"I understand. But this isn't over," he said. "We're just going to slow down a bit. And I'll prove myself to you…and to myself."

"All right," Malin said. She stood up and looked around the room. "I have to stop by the office today. I'm behind on my work, and I've got to get the gowns boxed up and sent back. Can we talk about this later?"

Thom nodded. "Why don't we have dinner tonight? I've got a little surprise for you."

"Not another pharmaceutical salesperson, I hope."

Thom laughed, then shook his head. "I'm never going to live that down, am I? We'll be eighty years old and you'll still be bringing it up."

"You looked so guilty," she said. "And you were kissing her!"

"No, no, she was kissing me."

"That's not possible."

"Sure it is," he said. "Go ahead. Try it. You kiss me and I won't kiss you back. You'll see what it's like."

"You can't help but react," she said.

"Try me."

Malin, never one to back down from a challenge, he knew, stood up beside the bed, then pulled him up alongside her. Her eyes fixed on his lips. She pushed up on her toes, wrapped her arms around his neck and pressed her lips to his. Though it was difficult, Thom did his best to maintain his composure. Her lips were soft and warm. Her tongue gently probed, not at all aggressive or demanding like Jennifer's kiss. As she moved her body against his, Thom felt his blood surge and his pulse increase.

Grabbing her shoulders, he gently pushed her back. He took in a ragged breath and smiled. "That's not exactly how it was. It wasn't as romantic, or so sweet. You need to be…cooler, more arrogant."

"Like this?"

She grabbed the back of his neck and yanked him down, their mouths meeting in a whirlwind of desire and demand. It was precisely how Jennifer had kissed him. Only now, with Malin, it felt entirely different— exciting and dangerous.

He cupped her face in his hands, molding her mouth to his. This was proof that he loved her, Thom thought to himself. No other woman had ever affected him this way. No one else had been able to stir his need with a simple kiss. A kiss from Malin was like a microcosm of sex—the contact, the caress, the penetration, the heat and warmth.

Suddenly she drew away, and Thom returned to reality. He looked down at Malin and gave her a sheepish grin. "Sorry. That wasn't the way it happened. You're just a lot better at kissing than she was."

"I have to go," Malin said. "I've got to set up new Twitter accounts for two of the players, and I've got tweets to approve. I haven't looked at my mail in about a week. And now that you've decided to go, I have to figure out how to handle the backlash from fans." She paused. "Do you think you would have fought to stay if we hadn't met and started seeing each other?"

He shrugged. "Maybe."

"I should have just minded my own business," Malin murmured.

"I'm glad you spoke with me that day. It meant a lot to me that you took my side." He reached out and grabbed her hand, then pulled her fingertips to his lips. "God, you were beautiful that day. Like a ray of pure sunshine."

"I have to go." Malin said again. She searched the room for something to wear, then finally grabbed a sundress that she'd stuffed into the dresser at the end of the bed.

She tossed the gown over her arm, gathered up her iPad and walked from the bedroom into the kitchen.

"I guess you're all set," Thom said.

A sudden panic set in, and he felt the need to keep her with him just a bit longer. For some reason, her leaving seemed like an ending, like he might never see her again. But that was ridiculous. They had dinner plans for the evening. "Would you like me to pick you up for dinner or do you want to meet here?"

"Can I call you?" Malin asked.

He nodded, then leaned forward to brush a kiss across her lips. The urge to confess his love for her nearly overwhelmed him again, but he bit back the words. What was wrong with him?

Thom walked her out to her car and helped her in. As she pulled away from the curb, he gave her a little wave.

This was what it would be like when they had to say goodbye for good in a few weeks. He'd pack up his truck and take off for New York. Only Malin would be the one standing on the curb and waving goodbye.

The office was busy when she arrived. The staff were working on another Sunday to put together the final preparations for the BlizzardCon fan convention, which opened on Friday. Usually Thom Quinn would have been one of the stars assigned to panel discussions and autograph sessions, but because of the trade possibilities, he'd been left out.

After she got her email down to a more manageable volume, she decided it was time to face the music. Her father's office door was open, and she knocked softly and peeked inside. Davis Pedersen looked up from his desk. "I expected you'd stop in to see me today," he said, leaning back in his leather chair.

"Do you have a few minutes?"

"I have an hour. Why don't we go get a sandwich? I need some lunch."

They walked back out into the heat of the summer day. Hers father's favorite lunch spot was an old diner that served all the rich, calorie-laden comfort foods that Malin's mother denied him at home.

They sat down at a booth, and the waitress handed them menus. Malin set hers down on the table and decided to begin the conversation. "Mama did a beautiful job with the benefit, didn't she?"

"She has a way with things like that. I sometimes think that I might have held her back by marrying her and turning her into a mother and a housewife."

Malin was stunned by his confession. Her father rarely indulged in self-examination. He was supremely confident in every move that he made, a quality that had allowed him to bring a struggling hockey franchise back from the brink of failure. "That's something I wouldn't have expected you to realize."

"I've never professed to understand women. And I didn't think that really mattered. Your mother loves me. There's no question about that. And I assumed that as long as I loved her and protected her and gave her a happy life, we'd be fine."

"And aren't you?" Malin asked.

"Yes. But life didn't really prepare me to raise a daughter. Sons were easy. But you have always been a puzzle to me."

"I'm not that complicated," Malin said. Her father had never been a very introspective man. But something had changed that, and it must have happened recently. "What brings this up now?"

"I suppose I realized it last night, when you confessed you were in love with Thom Quinn. I realized that at some point, you're going to leave your mother and me for a husband and a family of your own. And I've wasted all this time and never really gotten to know you or your skills. I regret that."

"I need to talk to you about Thom," Malin said. "He had second thoughts about New York, but now he's decided to take the trade."

"What happened?"

Malin reached for her water and took a slow slip, then shrugged. "It's just not working out as I'd hoped. Which is fine. I'm perfectly fine with it."

"I'm sorry, Linny. But the man has a reputation. I'm glad you've seen the light."

"No, that's not it. He's a good man, better than anyone even knows. Things are just complicated. With the trade and my job here and his... Well, he doesn't think he's good enough for me."

Her father seemed taken aback by the revelation. "Funny. I once felt that way with your mother. I was the very last man her father would have chosen for her. And he fought us all the way. But that only made your mother more determined. Sometimes I think she had more faith in me than I had in myself."

"That's the trouble. I'm not sure I completely trust that Thom has left The Beast completely behind."

"Is it him you don't believe in, or yourself?"

"What do you mean?"

"You came out here to prove yourself to me. This Beast project was supposed to open my eyes, wasn't it? Well, it might not have in the way you intended, but I do see you differently now, Malin. No matter what happens with Quinn, you've achieved a marketing coup, and all through social media. I'm not going to overlook your talents again. But whatever move you make next, I want you to make it because it's what *you* want to do. Understand?"

Malin wasn't sure she did, but just then the waitress came to take their order. Her father insisted that they share a chocolate malt, something the two of them used to do when she was very little.

"When did we stop going for malts?" Malin asked.

"I used to take you on Saturdays at lunch. I'd work at the office, your mother would drop you off after your ballet lessons and we'd go out for lunch. Then you started taking two ballet classes on Saturdays and I got busier with work, and we just let it go."

"Maybe we should start again," Malin suggested.

Davis reached out and place his hand over hers. "What do you want me to do about Thom Quinn? If you want him to stay, I'll cancel the trade. If you want him to go, I'll send him away."

"He's made the decision to go to New York, and I'm going to support him. He has his reasons, and I understand them."

Her father nodded. "Then it's settled."

"I suppose it is," Malin replied.

They spent the rest of their lunch chatting about the upcoming fan convention and about some new social media opportunities that Malin planned to use during the convention.

When they finished, her father paid the check, and they walked back to the team's offices. "I've been thinking that we need to find someone to handle your social media work. Talk to Ginny in Personnel and have her start advertising for your replacement."

"But I'm not going to New York," Malin said.

"No, you're going scouting first. And after that, I want you to work in player personnel. I want you to get a feel for how we handle our players, from the time we first spot them in the junior leagues to the time they step onto the ice with the Blizzard. If you're interested in learning the business, you're going to have to get your hands dirty."

"I am interested," Malin said, tears swimming in her eyes. "I'll work very hard for you, I promise."

When they got back to the office, Malin pitched in with getting the fan convention materials sorted and packaged. She was putting together the stacks of photos to be used for autographing when she came across a packet labeled with Thom's name. She pulled back the brown paper wrapping and withdrew a photo.

Malin smiled as she ran her fingers over the details of his handsome face. His hair was longer in the photo, and there was a fresh scar on his lower lip that had now faded almost completely, but it was an image of the man who'd slept beside her for the past few weeks.

"Malin?"

She turned and found Natalie standing beside her,

clutching a piece of paper tightly. "Hey, Natalie. How are you? Have you recovered from the benefit?"

"I—I wanted to apologize for that," Natalie said.

Malin frowned. "For what?"

"For the photo. I want to assure you that it was purely platonic, and the—"

"Stop!" Malin said. She pointed to a spot beside her on the floor. "Sit."

Natalie did as she was told, sitting primly, her hands folded in her lap. "I didn't want you to think I was trying to steal your boyfriend."

"Is that what you're worried about?" Malin laughed, pressing her hand to her lips and looking around to see if anyone in earshot had noticed. "He's not my boyfriend," she whispered.

"But I thought—"

"No, it's just not going to work out."

Natalie bent closer. "Then you wouldn't mind if I let a few people think that the photo of us dancing is, well, a little more romantic than it really is? My parents have been on my case to get me to settle down."

"Go for it," Malin said.

"He really is sweet. And I'm sorry that it didn't work out for you."

Malin pulled a photo from the package and handed it to Natalie. "You're going to need one of these," she said. "You can put it up on your refrigerator. And kiss it every morning."

Natalie giggled.

"Go ahead, give it a try," Malin urged. She held up her own photo of Thom and on the count of three, they kissed the shiny surfaces. In the end, they couldn't seem to stop laughing. All the emotions that Malin had held so tightly inside her didn't come out in tears, but in laughter.

She was in love with Thom Quinn. Tommy the Beast had stolen her heart. But the memory of what they'd shared was bittersweet. It had had an extraordinary beginning, but the end was near.

Could they make it work with such a big distance between them? Could she survive on just sweet summers?

She wiped the tears from her eyes and glanced over at Natalie. "I do have an important question to ask you."

"Anything."

"I'm going to be working in scouting and player personnel starting next month, and I need someone to take over new media. Would you be interested?"

Natalie stopped giggling for a moment, then clearly thought the job offer was part of the joke. "A new job and a new boyfriend, all in one day. What a lucky girl!"

"I'm serious. I'm moving on, and I'd be very happy if you took over the job."

As Natalie enthusiastically accepted, Malin felt tears gather her eyes. There were so many emotions rolling around inside of her, but she'd have to sort them out later. When she was alone.

9

A FEW WEEKS LATER, Malin sat in the center of Thom's bed, dressed in one of his old hockey jerseys and a pair of sagging socks. The weather outdoors seemed to match both of their moods—gray and restive. Dark clouds had gathered on the horizon. The weather service had issued a tornado warning, but there was no delaying Thom's departure.

She'd continued to live at his place over the last few weeks, but they had avoided talking about anything serious. And now Thom wished they'd at least had a few more discussions about what would happen when he drove away.

"Are you sure you have everything?" Malin asked.

He stood beside the bed, dressed in faded shorts and a loose T-shirt. His hair was still wet from the shower.

"I suppose if I've forgotten anything, you can send it to me. I've got sticks and the rest of my gear in the truck. There's still room for you," he teased. "Just a tiny little spot beneath the dash."

"Tempting," she said. "But you're going to have to find someone else to take care of your manly needs."

Thom sat down on the edge of the bed and pulled her into a kiss. "How many times do I have to tell you, Malin? You're the only one I want."

Malin threw herself into his arms and pushed him back into the soft mattress. Her lips found his, and she began a slow seduction that had always worked on him in the past. But Thom refused to join in, and when Malin drew away, he smiled at her.

"Sweetheart, I've already put the trip off three days. But now I've run out of time. Training camp starts the day after tomorrow, and most of the guys have been on the ice for weeks now."

"You've been skating," she said.

"I haven't done anywhere near the training I usually do. I've been a bit distracted this summer."

"And I suppose you're going to blame me if you have a slow start to the season?"

Malin crawled on top of him, her legs straddling his hips. Over the past few weeks they had desperately avoided any talk of the future by having as much sex as humanly possible.

She began to trail kisses down his chest, and Thom knew exactly where she was headed. He gently grabbed her waist and pulled her beneath him. "We have to stop," he said.

"I know," Malin said. "I'm all right. Really."

Thom bent down and kissed her, just a tiny taste before he crawled back off the bed. From the moment the trade had been announced, the clock had begun to tick on their relationship. He'd gone to BlizzardCon and tried to smooth over the anger of the fans. After that, he and Malin had filled every free moment with physical contact, whether it was holding hands or making love. But now it made the thought of leaving entirely impossible.

"How far will you drive today?"

"I'm not sure. I'm going to play it by ear. If I feel like going straight through, I will."

"I wish you wouldn't," Malin said. "Not without someone else there to keep you awake."

"All right, I promise to stop."

"And are they going to help you find an apartment?" she asked.

"They're putting me up in a hotel to start, and then I'll find a place to rent. I'm beginning to wonder if I should just stay in the hotel. I'd have room and laundry service and a maid to make the bed. That way, I'll save all my free time for missing you."

She smiled. "And you *will* miss me. I promise you that." Malin reached out and took his hands, then placed them on her hips. "All right, then, give me one more kiss goodbye and I'll let you go."

Her words brought an unexpected pain to his heart, and for a long moment, Thom couldn't breathe. This was it. When he'd gotten up this morning, Thom had decided that he would set the example and remain upbeat and unemotional, so he tried not to let his misery show. "So, you have a key. You'll check on the place every now and then. I've got someone to take care of the plants on the roof and shovel the snow in the winter."

"Can I come over every weekend and sleep in your bed?" she asked.

"I'm counting on it," he said. "I want to imagine you here, naked, between my sheets."

"Maybe I'll break my own rule and take a few pictures."

"Don't tease! One last thing. Will you walk me down?"

Malin nodded. She clasped her arms in front of her as if she were trying to keep her body from flying apart at the seams.

When she shuddered, Thom slipped his arms around her shoulders and pulled her close. "Are you cold?"

"No," she said. "Just scared."

When they got downstairs, Malin was trembling so much that he was forced to wrap both his arms around her and hold her against his chest.

"Don't worry," he whispered. "Everything will be all right. The fall will go so fast, and I'll be back home twice. Then there's the Christmas break and the all-star break. And just a few months after that, the season will be over and I'll be home for three months."

Malin nodded. He hooked her chin with his thumb and stole one last kiss. And then, summoning every ounce of will he possessed, he stepped back. "I love you, Malin."

Her eyes were wide and filled with tears, and with every step he took away from her, his heart felt as if it were being ripped out of his chest.

"I love you," she murmured.

He walked out the door, and she followed.

Thom took a ragged breath, and then another and another. By the time he slipped behind the wheel of his truck, he felt like he'd run a marathon. He took one last look at her slender figure standing on his front stoop, dressed only in an oversized Blizzard jersey.

Three months ago, he hadn't known her. And today she was the center of his universe. How the hell had that happened? And how was he going to live without her?

LIFE ON THE ROAD was an adventure that Malin had never expected to experience. And yet here she was, driving through a snowstorm to get to a college hockey game in North Dakota, where she would spend about an hour watching a promising young forward.

She'd started her new job at the beginning of the season, bouncing around the country, landing in obscure airports, driving rental cars across windswept highways, sitting in freezing-cold ice rinks, all in the hopes of finding a diamond in the rough before another team did.

It was all so awful, and yet Malin appreciated the chance to prove herself.

"I think we'll have enough time to check in to our motel before we go to the rink." She glanced over at Jimmy Callahan, one of the team scouts and her mentor for the month. The first part of her training involved shadowing each scout on staff. She had just two scouts after Jimmy before she could officially get off the road.

"What did you think of that Rowland kid?" Jimmy asked.

"I watched the film. He's a big kid, and he'd have to drop some weight if we're going to expect any kind of speed from him. His transitions are shaky at best, but he leads the conference in assists. Ultimately, he's a project, and I don't think he's for us."

Malin stared out the windshield at the worsening snowstorm, the flakes rushing at the car. The winter would have seemed almost endless, yet it ticked by, marked with regularly scheduled games that she caught on her computer. She couldn't help but follow Thom's own transition.

He was having a less than spectacular season so far. Though he tried hard, he just couldn't seem to adjust to the system in New York. He seemed distracted, flatfooted and slow. When asked in interviews, he'd blame himself and talk about what he was doing to get better. But Malin could see the frustration in his eyes, and she couldn't help but wonder if she was the real cause.

"I heard the Blizzard's management is planning on making a few more moves before the holiday. Any clues what they're planning to do?"

Nearly everyone in the organization knew that Malin was the owner's daughter. And though most might assume she had gotten her job through nepotism, once they worked with her, they saw that she put in the hours and the work to become a valuable part of the staff. She still felt she had a long way to go to prove herself, though. It seemed she had traded her mission of impressing her father for impressing everyone in the company.

But no one knew that she was involved with Thom Quinn. With the exception of a few trusted people, their affair was a deeply held secret. When his name came up in conversation, she nodded and acted as if her heart wasn't pounding for him.

At night, alone in her room, she'd strip off her clothes and crawl between the sheets and try to imagine his naked body curled up against hers. Sometimes she could make herself dream of him, and she'd wake up on the edge of release.

Early in the season, they'd talked on the phone nearly every night. But then, as things began to go wrong for him, he called less often. Malin knew she needed to give him space to work through his frustration. He'd been the one to choose New York, but it was becoming clear that it had been the wrong choice.

She tried to imagine where they'd be if he'd stayed. Would they still be wild for each other, the way they had been last summer? Or would the passion have cooled to a low burn like most relationships did? And while he'd been the one who'd ultimately decided to go, she'd been the one who'd refused to entertain any notion of a long-term relationship. She hadn't even told him she loved him until the day he left. Would things have been different had she said it earlier? Malin was left with a very long list of what-ifs.

An image of him danced in her head—broad shoulders, muscled chest, flat belly. She drew a deep breath and imagined the scent of his shampoo. And then the feel of his hair between her fingers.

By the time she realized the car was sliding, it was too late to recover. Startled, Malin yanked the wheel to the left as the car spun on the snow-covered highway. The back bumper hit the snowbank at the side of the road, and the car came to a stop.

Her breath, which she'd been holding tightly during the spin, burst from her throat. She looked over at Jimmy, whose normally ruddy complexion had turned ghost white. "Are you all right?"

He nodded. "I need a drink."

"We're almost to the motel. We'll check in, you can relax for a bit and then we'll go the arena."

Jimmy nodded.

"Sorry about that," Malin said. "I should have been paying closer attention."

"Do you want me to drive?" Jimmy asked.

"I'll be fine," she said. But would she? What if things were only going to get worse? What if Thom decided to put both of them out of their misery and end things for good? If that was the case, she needed to know.

She and Jimmy checked in to their motel at six thirty with an hour left until puck drop. The campus and the hockey arena were only about a mile away, so she took a hot shower, then wrapped herself in her thick terry robe and sat down on the bed.

She picked up her phone and scrolled through her apps until she found Thom's schedule. He wasn't playing tonight but he was on the road, staying at a hotel in Winnipeg. Her breath caught and she groaned. She was about a two-hour drive from Winnipeg. She was just a couple of hours away from his warm body and sweet kisses.

Malin dialed his number. When he answered, she curled up beneath the covers and closed her eyes, trying to imagine what he was wearing. "Hi," she said. "Are you busy?"

"Nope. Just hanging out in my room, catching up on some reading. I didn't expect to hear from you tonight."

"Guess where I am?"

"I don't know. My bed?"

"No. I'm not home. I'm on the road. Just a few hours south of where you are, actually. Grand Forks, North Dakota."

"Two hours?"

"Well, maybe a bit more. One-hundred forty-five miles. That's the closest we've been in weeks."

"I'm not sure if that's good or bad."

"It's snowing here," Malin said. "And it's so cold. Maybe you could sneak out of the hotel, steal a car and come visit me."

"That would be against the rules," he said. "And I'm strictly a good boy now. Maybe you could drive up here. We could spend the night together in my room."

"I have to watch a game. And the storm is getting worse."

"God, I hate this," he said. "I feel like we're drifting around on two boats and the currents are pulling us apart. I can see you, but I can't touch you."

"I understand exactly what you mean. I knew long-distance would be difficult, but I didn't think it would be this bad."

"Christmas is only a month away. We can last until then," Thom said. "Don't give up."

"I won't if you won't."

"There's something else I need to tell you, and I don't want you to get upset."

"I'm already upset," Malin said. "What is it?"

"I'm hearing whispers about another trade."

Silence spun out between them, and Malin's eyes filled with tears. "Another trade? Where? Do you know?"

"Montreal."

She drew a deep breath but couldn't cover the sob that escaped. "I have to go. I'll talk to you tomorrow, all right?"

"Malin, wait. We need to—"

She switched off the phone, then tossed it onto the bed before pulling the covers over her head. Malin let the tears flow, releasing all the emotions she'd been holding on to so tightly since he'd walked out of her life nearly three months before.

She couldn't live like this. She didn't have the patience or the fortitude to love a man and not be with him. They'd be together for a few days around the holidays, sure, but then it would go back to the same old routine for another four months.

Cursing softly, Malin picked up her phone and dialed Natalie's number. "Hi, Nat."

"Malin! How's life on the road? Where are you?"

"Grand Forks, North Dakota."

"Exciting," she said.

"Could you to do a little snooping for me? There are rumors of a trade going down between New York and Montreal. Don't be obvious about it. And don't let on that it came from me."

"Is it Thom?"

"Maybe."

"Montreal. Two trades in one season. That's not good."

"How is the job going?"

"All right. We've had a few fires to put out. One off-color joke made by one player, one naked woman with another player, and two accusations of animal cruelty involving a goldfish. Other than that, it's been all right."

"Hang in there. I'll be back in the office the day after tomorrow, and I'll help you out if you need me to."

"Thanks, Malin. I'll see you soon."

Malin glanced at the clock on her phone, then closed her eyes. She had another fifteen minutes to herself. She could lie in bed and think about all the things that were going wrong. Or she could get dressed and do the job she'd been assigned to do.

She sat up and swung her legs off the bed. Grabbing her bag, she searched through the contents until she found her long underwear. Malin couldn't help but laugh.

A few years ago, she'd dressed in designer clothes and worked for a top fashion magazine. Now she was putting on her long underwear to attend a college hockey game. Then again, a few months ago she was in the midst of a wildly passionate affair with a bad boy hockey player. Now she was all alone.

She'd been happiest on those days with Thom when she hadn't been trying to improve his reputation or impress her father. When they'd just been two people in love.

How had she lost sight of that? When her father had blindsided her with news that Thom had accepted the trade to New York, the doubts had started creeping in. Doubts about Thom. Doubts about how they could ever make a relationship work. She'd accused him of not fighting for their relationship, but had she fought for it? She hadn't even admitted to Natalie that they were a couple.

Malin looked around the room and took in the peeling wallpaper, the hideous motel bedspread and the stained carpet. What was she doing here? What was she trying to prove?

Her father had asked her if it was really Thom she didn't trust, or herself. He'd told her to do only what she wanted to do. But she'd never allowed herself any chance to do any proper soul searching. She'd been too busy impressing her father, then her new colleagues.

That ended now. She was done worrying about what other people would think. She was done hiding her head in the sand. It was time to fight for what she wanted.

"IS IT MONTREAL?"

Thom glanced over at his teammate, Eddie Cooper,

and shrugged. "Still not sure. I called my agent and he said it was all very hush-hush."

He and Eddie had played on the Olympic hockey team five years ago and had also spent two seasons together with the Blizzard. Eddie had been the first one to welcome him to New York, and since then they'd rekindled their friendship.

"You have a no-trade clause, don't you?"

"Not on this contract. We switched to a modified trade. Ten teams. But Montreal isn't on the list. Maybe it's not me."

"I don't know, man. Your name keeps coming up. I'm really sorry. I think you're good for this team. You bring a lot of wisdom."

"Thanks," Thom said. "I hope I don't have to go. I'm just getting used to the system here."

"Any plans for Thanksgiving?" Eddie asked. "My family is staying in town. If you're not leaving, you're welcome to join us."

"I don't have plans."

"Not going to see the girl?"

"No, she has to work the day after."

"What does she do?" Eddie asked.

Thom hadn't told any of his new teammates about Malin. He'd referred to a girlfriend in vague terms that no one seemed to question. "She's in marketing. She travels a lot for work."

"How is she going to take it if you end up in Montreal?"

"I'm not going," he said. "This time, I'm putting a stop to it."

"This time?"

"You've got my number," Thom said. "Text me the details on Thanksgiving. And let me know if I can bring anything."

Frank Pritzker, one of the assistant coaches, walked into the locker room and nodded at Thom. "Coach wants to see you."

"Right now?" Thom asked.

"Yep, right now."

Thom glanced over at Eddie. "Here we go."

"Call me and let me know what happens," Eddie said. "Good luck."

The head coach, John Norris, was waiting for him in his office. "Come on in and shut the door," he said, his voice gruff, his expression unreadable.

"Just tell me where," Thom said. "I've heard about the trade."

"Your agent is waiting for you outside. He'll explain the whole thing. They've arranged a car that will take you to the airport. All you have to do is gather up your gear. We sent someone to your hotel room to pack up, and that's already been loaded on the plane." Norris stood and held out his hand. "It's been a pleasure, Thom. Wish you could have stayed with us a little longer."

"Why couldn't I?" Thom asked.

Norris chuckled softly. "We got an offer we couldn't refuse."

"Thanks, Coach." Thom walked back into the locker room and grabbed his duffel, then began to throw his gear inside. The equipment manager brought in a bag with his sticks and gloves, then shook his hand and wished him luck. As he walked out of the practice rink, Thom couldn't help but wonder how Malin would take the latest news. He already felt like he was on thin ice with her. She'd always been cagey about defining their relationship, and the distance had only eaten away at her confidence.

Maybe he'd been wrong to leave her. He could have stayed in Minneapolis and convinced her that she could trust him. He could have fought harder for his spot there. But he'd taken the easy way out. He'd been afraid that he wasn't equipped to love her the way she deserved to be loved. He certainly wasn't shining in that department lately.

Jack was waiting at the door, and he waved as Thom approached. "What the hell is this all about, Jack?"

Jack grabbed the bag of sticks. "We'll talk in the car."

A black Lincoln Town Car waited at the curb. The driver stepped out and helped them put the bags in the trunk before opening the passenger door for Thom and Jack. They slid into the comfortable interior, Jack taking the seat beside Thom. The door slammed shut and Jack leaned forward to shut the privacy screen.

"What the hell is going on?" Thom said.

"That's what I've been asking myself all day," Jack said.

"Why didn't you call and let me know this was going down?"

"Because I didn't have any answers," Jack said.

"They didn't give me any information until all the deals were done."

"Am I going to Montreal?"

"No," Jack said. "You're headed back to Minneapolis."

Thom gasped. "What?"

"You heard me. The Blizzard got you back as part of a three-way trade. And they've offered a second signing bonus to your original contract."

Thom shook his head. "I don't get it."

"I don't, either. They're going to have to explain what the hell they're thinking."

It couldn't be this simple, could it? Thom mused. Taking the New York trade had been a colossal mistake. And now, out of the blue, that mistake had been fixed. He was going home. He was going back to Malin and to a life that was as close to perfection as he'd ever experienced.

He pulled out his phone, anxious to call her and tell her the news. But when he rang her number, she didn't pick up. Frowning, Thom tried a text, but after a few minutes, there was still no response.

He glanced out the window and noticed they were headed west, across the Hudson and away from the city. "Where are we going?"

"From what I understand, Pedersen is sending the corporate jet. The Blizzard's playing tonight in Minneapolis, and they want you on the ice. I think we're heading to the airport in Teterboro."

Thom sank back into the leather seat and closed his eyes. It was hard to believe that he'd be sleeping in his own bed tonight. He wanted to believe that Malin would be there waiting for him. But she'd struggled with their separation. For all he knew, she was waiting to see him in person before she ended things.

"Thanks for getting me back home, Jack. I really appreciate it."

"Don't thank me," he said. "You should probably thank Davis Pedersen."

Thom looked out the window and watched as the scenery passed by. "I'll do that."

Thirty minutes later, the Town Car pulled up to a hangar on the outskirts of the airport. The driver helped Thom remove his bags from the trunk, and a steward appeared to help load the bags into the cargo hold of the jet.

Jack said goodbye and got back in the car. Thom headed up the steps to greet the pilot, who was waiting for him by the cockpit. "Good evening, Mr. Quinn. Welcome aboard."

"Thank you," he said.

The steward closed the door as the pilot returned to the cockpit. Thom glanced around the luxurious cabin. The team usually traveled in a nicely appointed charter jet, but this was way beyond their travel accommodations.

"Can I get you anything to drink, Mr. Quinn?"

Thom looked up at the steward. "A water? I'm playing tonight, so I can't have anything to drink."

"I could make you a sandwich. We have turkey, ham and beef."

"Turkey would be great," he said.

"We've got another passenger. I'll go get her order and be right back with your drink."

Thom peered around the edge of the seat, wondering who else was on the jet. Once they took off, he'd wander back and introduce himself.

Thom watched out the window as they taxied out to the runway. A few seconds later, the plane began to accelerate and then gently left the ground. The engines roared as they climbed, the snowy landscape of New York State stretching out below them.

The steward returned with his sandwich and drink, setting them both on a tray that flipped out from the arm of the seat. "If there's anything else you need, just push that button," he said, indicating a button above Thom's head.

Thom nodded and pulled out his phone to try Malin's number. But as it rang, he heard a soft echo of her ringtone.

"Hello?"

"Malin?"

"Thom?"

"Where have you been? I've been trying to call but you didn't answer."

"I'm on a plane back to Minneapolis," she said. "Where are you?"

"You're not going to believe this," Thom said, "but I'm on a plane back to Minneapolis, too. I've been traded again. To the Blizzard." A long silence met his declaration. "Malin? Did you hear me? I'm coming home."

"I heard you just fine."

Thom twisted around to find Malin standing behind his seat, her arms braced on the headrest, her chin resting on her hands. He got up and knelt on the aisle seat, pulling her into a long and delicious kiss.

When he finished with her lips, he moved on to her cheeks and then her eyes and her nose and her chin, raining kisses all over her pretty face. Malin tipped her head back, laughing, and Thom attacked her neck.

"When did you find out?" he asked.

"I accused you once of not fighting to stay. But I realized I hadn't done much fighting for what I wanted, either. It wasn't you I didn't trust, but myself. So I called my dad and told him my idea. He recognized that it would be good for the team, and he made it happen. I want us to be together, Thom. As in a real couple. I want to tell the world that I love you." She paused. "If that's all right with you, of course?"

He kissed her again, cupping her face in his hands. "Of course it is. Malin, I never should have left you. It's the stupidest move I've ever made in my entire life. And I've made a lot of stupid moves. I just got scared that I wouldn't be able to make you happy."

"You do make me happy," Malin said.

"Happy forever," he said. "I want us to be together, too. But I want an entire lifetime. I want to know that when I wake up in the morning, you're going to be right there beside me. And I want to introduce you to my brothers and my grandmother. They're going to love you."

"I want that, too," Malin said. "I've missed you so much."

"God, you're so damn beautiful."

Laughing, Malin crawled over the tall seat back, then sank onto Thom's lap. He pulled her close, nuzzling his face into her neck.

Malin drew back, ran her fingers over his chin and found a fresh bruise. "What's this?"

"I got hit by a puck last week."

"I'm going to be glad when you decide to retire."

"I've been giving that a lot of thought, actually, and I've realized what I'm going to do after hockey. I want to start a nonprofit to help troubled or underprivileged kids get into hockey camps." She pulled away from him slightly and stared at him. "Malin? What do you think?"

"I think that's a wonderful idea. You'll be great at it."

"Yeah? Thanks."

"Plus, once you get off the ice, there'll be less abuse to your pretty face," she said with a grin.

"What about my pretty body?" Thom asked. "I've got a sore shoulder, a tweaked hamstring and a twisted ankle."

"How are your hands?" she asked.

"Good."

"And what about your lips? Do they still work?"

Thom chuckled. "Yes."

"And the manly parts?" she asked. "Are they functioning properly?"

"Which parts are the manly ones?"

Malin wriggled in his lap, creating a warm friction against the front of his jeans. He responded almost instantly, his shaft pushing against the faded fabric. "I think they're doing just fine."

"Have you ever done the mile-high thing?"

"Believe it or not, that's one thing I've never tried."

Malin grinned, pleased with his answer. "Then we have to try it."

"What about the steward?"

"I told him to forget the water and asked him not to come unless we call him," Malin explained.

"I have a game tonight," he said. "I usually don't have sex before a game. It's just a silly superstition, but I've never broken it."

"Well, if you can't have sex with me, then I'll have sex with you and you can watch. You won't even have to move. I'll do everything."

Thom laughed. "You're serious? You want to seduce me on this plane? Your father's plane?"

She reached in her pocket and pulled out a long string of condoms. "I came prepared. I've been thinking about this all the way from South Dakota. And I'm pretty sure it's going to be much better in real life than it is in my imagination."

"I've been using my imagination a lot over the past few months," he murmured. Thom reached for the buttons on her shirt and undid them one at a time. "I guess we'd better get started."

Malin stood up in front of him and began to take off her clothes. "Then unfasten your seat belt, mister. It's going to be a very bumpy ride."

As Thom watched Malin complete her impromptu striptease, he realized what his time away from her had accomplished. There was no doubt anymore, no questions about whether he was capable of loving her.

He'd loved her from the moment he'd met her, and nothing that life tossed their way would ever break that bond. She was the only woman in the world made especially for him. And he'd been lucky enough to find her.

* * * * *

#903 COWBOY UNTAMED

Thunder Mountain Brotherhood

by Vicki Lewis Thompson

Potter Sapphire Ferguson has been burned too many times. No more relationships with artists! But sculptor Grady Magee ignites her passion—and might just change her mind—with his cowboy soul.

#904 HER SEAL PROTECTOR

Uniformly Hot!

by Jillian Burns

When hardened Navy SEAL Clay Bellamy agrees to act as her bodyguard, quiet executive banker Gabby Diaz is determined to take more chances...especially given how hot Clay makes her feel.

#905 WILD FOR YOU

Made in Montana

by Debbi Rawlins

Spencer Hunt, a rancher living outside Blackfoot Falls, Montana, just wants to be left in peace. But filmmaker Erin Murphy wants to shoot on his land—and she won't leave him alone!

#906 TRIPLE SCORE

The Art of Seduction

by Regina Kyle

When good-girl ballerina Noelle Nelson meets bad-boy shortstop Jace Monroe, not even the injuries that landed them both in rehab can stop their sizzling attraction. But is this an illicit affair or something deeper?

REQUEST YOUR FREE BOOKS!
2 FREE NOVELS PLUS 2 FREE GIFTS!

HARLEQUIN®

Blaze

red-hot reads!

YES! Please send me 2 FREE Harlequin® Blaze® novels and my 2 FREE gifts (gifts are worth about $10). After receiving them, if I don't wish to receive any more books, I can return the shipping statement marked "cancel." If I don't cancel, I will receive 4 brand-new novels every month and be billed just $4.74 per book in the U.S. or $5.21 per book in Canada. That's a savings of at least 14% off the cover price. It's quite a bargain. Shipping and handling is just 50¢ per book in the U.S. and 75¢ per book in Canada.* I understand that accepting the 2 free books and gifts places me under no obligation to buy anything. I can always return a shipment and cancel at any time. Even if I never buy another book, the two free books and gifts are mine to keep forever.

150/350 HDN GH2D

Name _____ (PLEASE PRINT)

Address _____ Apt. #

City _____ State/Prov. _____ Zip/Postal Code

Signature (if under 18, a parent or guardian must sign)

Mail to the **Reader Service:**
IN U.S.A.: P.O. Box 1867, Buffalo, NY 14240-1867
IN CANADA: P.O. Box 609, Fort Erie, Ontario L2A 5X3

Want to try two free books from another line?
Call 1-800-873-8635 or visit www.ReaderService.com.

* Terms and prices subject to change without notice. Prices do not include applicable taxes. Sales tax applicable in N.Y. Canadian residents will be charged applicable taxes. Offer not valid in Quebec. This offer is limited to one order per household. Not valid for current subscribers to Harlequin Blaze books. All orders subject to credit approval. Credit or debit balances in a customer's account(s) may be offset by any other outstanding balance owed by or to the customer. Please allow 4 to 6 weeks for delivery. Offer available while quantities last.

Your Privacy—The Reader Service is committed to protecting your privacy. Our Privacy Policy is available online at www.ReaderService.com or upon request from the Reader Service.

We make a portion of our mailing list available to reputable third parties that offer products we believe may interest you. If you prefer that we not exchange your name with third parties, or if you wish to clarify or modify your communication preferences, please visit us at www.ReaderService.com/consumerchoice or write to us at Reader Service Preference Service, P.O. Box 9062, Buffalo, NY 14240-9062. Include your complete name and address.

HB15

"Lady, you and I generate a lot of heat. You can head home to catch up on paperwork, but that's not going to change anything."

"Maybe not." She shoved her hands into her pockets and clutched her keys as a reminder that she was leaving. Just because he thought her surrender was inevitable didn't mean he was right. But she could feel that heat he was talking about melting her resistance. "I need to go." She started to turn away.

"Hang on for a second." He lightly touched her arm.

The contact sent fire through her veins. "What for?" She turned back to him and saw the intent before he spoke the words.

"A kiss."

"No, that would be—"

"Only fair. I've been imagining kissing you ever since I drove away three weeks ago. If you don't want to take it beyond that point, I'll abide by that decision." He smiled. "What's one little kiss?"

A mistake. "I guess that would be okay."

"Not a very romantic answer." He drew her into his arms and lowered his head. "But good enough."

The velvet caress of his mouth was every bit as spectacular as she'd imagined. If she stuck to her guns, this would never happen again, so it seemed criminal to waste a single second of kissing Grady Magee. She hugged him close as he worked his magic. She'd figured the man could kiss, but she hadn't known the half of it. He started slow, tormenting her with gentle touches that made her ache for more.

When he finally settled in, she opened to him greedily, desperately wanting the stroke of his tongue. Kissing him was exactly what she'd been trying to avoid, but when he cupped her bottom and drew her against the hard ridge of his cock, she forgot why she'd been so reluctant.

Wouldn't a woman have to be crazy to reject this man? Wrapped in his strong arms and teased with his hot kisses, she craved the pleasure he promised.

Taking his mouth from hers, he continued to knead her bottom with his strong fingers. "Still think we should nip this thing in the bud?"

Don't miss COWBOY UNTAMED
by Vicki Lewis Thompson, available in August 2016
wherever Harlequin® Blaze® books and ebooks are sold.

www.Harlequin.com

HBEXP0716

Reading Has Its Rewards

Earn **FREE BOOKS!**

Register at **Harlequin My Rewards** and submit your Harlequin purchases from wherever you shop to earn points for free books and other exclusive rewards.

Plus submit your purchases from now till May 30th for a chance to win a $500 Visa Card*.

Visit **HarlequinMyRewards.com** today

MYR16R1

7644

HARLEQUIN®
A *Romance* FOR EVERY MOOD™

Love the Harlequin book you just read?

Your opinion matters.

Review this book on your favorite book site, review site, blog or your own social media properties and share your opinion with other readers!